THE TAU CETI TRANSMUTATION

ALEX P. BERG

BATDOG PRESS
KNOXVILLE, TN

The Tau Ceti Transmutation/ Alex P. Berg — 1st ed.
ISBN 978-1-942274-07-0

1

I sighed as I finished yet another game of Smashblocks on my Brain.

Paige spoke in the back of my mind as the score flashed before my eyes. *Over fourteen point six billion. Not too shabby. That's one of your top five scores of all time, if I'm not mistaken.*

"Don't say it," I told Paige as I leaned back in my office chair.

Say what? Her voice dripped fake innocence.

I rapped my fingers on my desk. "That I'm pathetic. That I'm a loser. That I'm wasting my life playing these mind-dulling games."

Me? said Paige. *I'd never say any of that, Rich.*

I scoffed. Opportunities for sarcasm and belittlement rarely passed Paige by untouched, but to be fair, most of that was my fault. When I'd first initialized her, I'd chosen two primary personality parameters to help define her. I'd gone with bubbly and cynical.

While the result was *interesting*, to say the least, I sometimes regretted my flippant choice, but what could I do about it? I couldn't exactly tell Paige to take a hike. She was as much a part of me as my legs or my heart. And besides, I needed her to help run my Brain—the cybernetic implant that connected the near-infinite collected knowledge of the known sentient races directly into my gray matter. My Brain also interfaced with my central nervous system and sensory organs, allowing me to see, hear, smell, taste, and experience events the unconnected could only dream of.

I mostly used it to play Smashblocks and watch vids of dogs jumping on trampolines.

Paige snickered in the back of my mind. I let her mocking wash over me, placating myself with the knowledge that I was the only one who had to deal with her unique blend of wit and sass. Paige didn't really exist, you see. She was a digital imprint—a unique representation of a consciousness created by an enormous, hulking pile of servenets in a bunker somewhere in the bowels of Pylon Alpha, the capital city of Tau Ceti e, or Cetie as it was referred to colloquially. The servenets cultivated a different, tailored personality for every individual with a Brain. Instead of Paige, other people with Brains interacted with Bobs or Sallys or Qrtyfyls, depending on linguistic and cultural preferences.

Of course, I didn't *have* to suffer Paige's snappy retorts or her implications that I was a loser. I could send a request to the servenets to reconfigure her interactivity parameters at any time, but doing so would wipe out the fiery personality I'd spent a lifetime nurturing. Doing so, in my eyes, would be akin to murder. It would be like me taking an electromagnetic scrambler to Carl's computational core.

"I don't think Paige was implying you're a stain on society," said Carl as he crossed his legs.

I glanced at the slender, sharp-featured android sitting in the chair across from my desk, his medium-length blond hair perfectly coiffed in a factory-optional, mousse-heavy sweep cut. His given name was Carlton Weatherby, but I just called him Carl. My grandfather had purchased him a couple centuries ago when RAAI Corp first came out with their luxury line, envisioning him as an all-purpose manservant. Grandpappy had bequeathed him to me upon his death, but I found Carl's intellect and robotic skill set were wasted on buffing silverware. Instead, I'd purchased a buffbot for that, and Carl followed me around as my de facto partner.

Carl glanced at me from his perch on the velour sofa chair, the look on his face a mixture of uncertainty and concern. Despite his ability to interface directly with Paige through my Brain, he couldn't read my mind. I didn't let Paige share absolutely *everything* with him—just most of it.

"I feel like there's an unspoken *but* you wanted to add to the end of that sentence," I said.

Carl shifted uncomfortably. He was very sensitive to my emotional state. He couldn't help it. It was part of his programming.

"Go on. Spit it out," I said.

"Well," said Carl. "It's just that... perhaps it's time to admit this latest *enterprise* of yours hasn't succeeded in quite the fashion you'd hoped."

I glanced across the office to my front door. The words etched into the frosted glass were reversed from my vantage point, but I could still read them.

RICH WEED
PREMIUM INVESTIGATIVE SERVICES

"What are you trying to say?" I asked. "That I'm a failure? Because if so, that's a rather shortsighted viewpoint. I wasn't particularly suited to kickboxing or flightwing instruction or Brain app design either, but I gave all of those a fair shot before moving on to something else."

"Yes," said Carl. "But at least in those endeavors you actually received some level of business on a regular basis."

"We've had clients," I said.

Carl raised an eyebrow.

In a little over a standard galactic year since I'd established my latest venture, we'd had a grand total of three cases. Two had involved tracking down missing cats, and the third had revolved around a piece of missing jewelry that had eventually turned up outside the client's apartment complex embedded in a dog turd.

"Alright, maybe you have a point," I said. "But I'm no spring chicken. I can't keep zipping around on flightsuits or taking kicks for a living anymore."

While the first part of that is true, said Paige, *the second part is only accurate from a historical perspective, and you know it.*

I was eighty-five, but thanks to advances in medical technology and GenBorn's proprietary nanobot-driven rejuvenation services, I didn't look a standard galactic day older than an unmodified human at thirty. No one who enrolled in GenBorn's services did until they hit about the quarter millennia mark. At that point, even nanobots couldn't keep the corporeal self from falling apart. Of course, I also worked out regularly—a holdover from my kickboxing days—but I was fairly sure it was mostly the nanobots that kept me looking fresh.

"To be fair, you don't *need* to do much of anything," said Carl. "Between the revenue you generate off the land lease bequeathed to you by your great-grandfather and the annual government work stipend, you accrue far more income than you need to get by. This enterprise is purely for entertainment purposes. My point was that, if we're to apply ourselves to an occupation where we provide a service to the public, we should try to find one that has some demand—ideally one that puts your skills to good use."

"Like what?" I asked.

"Well, that depends on your skill set," said Carl.

"You've known me my entire life," I said. "I'd think you'd know my strengths and weaknesses pretty well by now."

"I do," said Carl. "But I was hoping you'd been keeping something secret from me for the last eighty-five years."

I tilted my head. "Why?"

"Because given my knowledge of your skills, talents, and attributes, I'm drawing a blank as to what profession you'd thrive at."

I frowned. "I think your compassion regulator is malfunctioning. You're not making me feel particularly sunny."

"I always try to be supportive, but not if the cost is a fictitious reality," said Carl. "It's better for your long term health and wellness for me to be honest."

I leaned back in my chair and ran a hand over my finger-length hair. Ever since I'd started my detective business, I'd taken to styling it with pomade. It added a glossy sheen to my matte black follicles which I thought gave me an air of debonairness, but I sometimes wondered if others thought it made me look unclean. I sighed as I dropped my hand back down.

Paige took note of my mood. *Perhaps you could try a career in comedy.*

I raised an eyebrow. "You think I'm funny?"

How funny you are is immaterial, Paige said. *You just need people to laugh at you. That seems to happen with relative frequency.*

"I'll have you know—"

A thumping sound interrupted my repartee—three rhythmic knocks in short succession.

"Did anyone else hear that?" I asked.

That's a rather silly question to pose, said Paige, *seeing as my input feed consists of the collated total of your own sensory experiences.*

"What I meant by that was if anyone knew what the sound was," I said. "Hopefully the landlord didn't rent the upstairs unit to a tap studio. He knows how much I hate syncopated musical arrangements."

"Nothing quite so conspiratorial, I think." Carl nodded his head toward the frosted glass showpiece that fronted my office. "It would appear someone's at the door."

A shadow on the other side of the door seemed to prove Carl's point.

I nearly did a double take, not only because the evidence suggested I might actually have a customer waiting to speak with me, but also because there appeared to be a real live flesh and blood—or possibly transistors and synthetics—individual waiting outside my office. Most people, whether human, alien, or droid, opted to communicate almost entirely via Brain messaging, so having a face-to-face visit was something of an anomaly.

The triple knock sounded again, and I waved hastily toward Carl. "Alright. This is it. Remember, we're a real professional investigative service. Stress that we have a 100% success rate in our cases—"

"All three of them..." said Carl.

"—and above all, play it cool."

As if we're the ones who need the soothing, said Paige.

My digital Brain companion was right. I took a deep breath to calm my nerves before speaking in my best measured, commanding voice. "Come in."

2

The door blinked open. Behind it stood a woman with voluminous, curly strawberry blond hair that orbited her head at a stratospheric length. Long lashes curled over eyelids heavily painted a bright goldenrod, and an off-white Spandette crop top and pants combination stuck to her skin like glue.

My breath caught in my throat. Her beauty transcended normal human limits—even accounting for the extensive prenatal genetic manipulation she undoubtedly underwent. I briefly wondered if she was even human, but her short stature and muscular build quickly put that question to rest.

Droids were universally fabricated to Earth standards of beauty—tall, lithe, and thin—making them visibly different from those of us who heralded from Cetie's warm soils. Due to Cetie's higher gravitational pull than Earth's, humans born and bred on the fourth world orbiting Tau Ceti tended to be shorter and denser, both in terms of skeletal structure and musculature. At a meter seventy-five, I was considered tall for a Cetiean, while the beauty outside my office was a much more average meter sixty.

The woman stood just inside the doorframe, casting her sky blue eyes my way. "Excuse me, are you Mr....Weed?"

I ran my tongue across my lips as I stood. "Um, yes. That's right. Rich Weed, of Rich Weed's Premium Investigative Services, at your service, Miss."

I didn't know her age, but that didn't affect my choice of honorific. One of the side effects of youth-prolonging rejuvenative medical technology was its effect on grammar. Now, all men and women, regardless of age or marital status, were Mr. and Miss.

"And you're a private investigator?" she asked.

"Correct," I said. "But I'm not *a* private investigator. I'm a *premium* investigator."

The lady in bioengineered breathable stretch fabric raised an eyebrow. "And what does that entail, exactly?"

I scratched the back of my neck. "An attention to detail, a focus on customer satisfaction, a money back guarantee of services rendered, and...well, that's about it. Honestly, I added the 'premium' part to distinguish myself from those other hack investigators out there."

"Oh," said the woman. "Well, I'm not sure that's necessary. When I queried the biz listings for private investigators, yours was the only name that appeared."

"Really? I guess that means Fredrickson and Sons went out of business." I glanced at Carl. "Did you know about that?"

He shrugged.

A quick check tells me Mr. Fredrickson passed away, said Paige, *and based on their social media profiles, his sons apparently repurposed his office into a hookah lounge. So it appears you are, in fact, the only investigator left in the listings.*

As I mulled over my newfound monopoly on Cetie's investigative operations, the woman at the door motioned toward my desk and spoke. "May I?"

"Where are my manners? Yes, please, come in." I gestured to the empty lounge across from my desk.

The stunner undulated over, setting her rock hard body—one that was even more chiseled than most—down in the plush chair. "Thank you," she said. "You know, I have to admit, when I saw your business in the listings, I wasn't sure what I'd find. I thought it might be a joke."

"What? Why?" I asked as I sat back down.

"Well, is that your real name?" She jerked her thumb toward the frosted glass.

"Rich is short for Richard, but yes," I said.

"And you're a private *detective?*"

I nodded.

The woman raised an eyebrow. "And you don't find the humor in that?"

"Don't bother," said Carl. "I've tried to break it to him gently on more than one occasion, but it doesn't quite seem to go through. I don't know if it's a conscious refusal to understand or if he's simply wired differently—figuratively speaking, of course. I'm the android, not him. I'm Carlton, but the way." He stuck out a hand. "I'm Mr. Weed's partner—of sorts."

"Valerie. Valerie Meeks." The woman shook hands with Carl.

I gave them both a slit-eyed look. "I'm not entirely sure what the two of you are insinuating, but I'll have you know I come from a long line of distinguished Weeds, all the way back to my great-grandpappy Dillinger Weed."

"Wait, really?" asked Valerie. "*Dillinger* Weed?"

"That's right," I said. "He was a weed farmer—the recreational kind, not the thorns and thistles type."

Valerie and Carl shared looks again. Carl shrugged. I cast a glance at Valerie and her skin-tight attire and felt my blood pressure rise, and not in the fun, localized way I normally experienced when impossibly attractive women showed any sort of interest in me.

Paige popped back into my thoughts before I could make a fool of myself. *You might want to revisit the words on your mind, Rich. Berating your first customer in months isn't the best of entrepreneurial strategies.*

Valerie didn't give me a chance to show off my people skills. Before I could speak, she pointed to a bronze bust sitting on the corner of my desk, angled inward to face me. "Is that you?"

I nodded. "Yes. I commissioned it to remind myself of my successes as a kick boxer. I needed something for my desk. It's rather barren, otherwise."

I expected a remark about my obvious narcissism, but instead Valerie replied with a simple, "That's cute."

I blinked, banishing away the last remnants of my frustration. "Oh. Well...thanks, I guess. So, Miss Meeks, how can I help you today?"

"Ah, yes," Valerie said. "Well, I have a rather interesting...*situation* I need assistance with, and I'm not sure where else to turn."

"Well, you're in luck," I said. "Interesting is my middle name."

Valerie raised an eyebrow. "I find that hard to believe. Now, something that plays humorously off your last name, on the other hand..."

I threw my hands in the air. "You got me. My parents didn't name me Richard Interesting Weed. They gave me a far more ridiculous middle name—Stanley."

Valerie tilted her head and peered at me askance, a smile creeping across her lips. "You're funny, Mr. Weed."

Her smile drew my eyes, which was probably for the best, seeing as I'd been lavishing far too much attention on her midriff and cleavage. "Tell it to my Brain. She thinks I'm a drip. And please, call me Rich. But let's not get distracted from your query. Why don't you tell me more about this situation of yours."

"Very well, Rich," said Valerie. "I'd like your help investigating a break-in."

"A B and E, eh?" I said. "Did you contact the police?"

"I did," said Valerie.

"And they weren't able to help you?"

She shook her head.

I snapped my fingers as the revelation hit me. "I see. Someone busted into your place and stole something, but those buffoons at the precinct couldn't find what was taken and now you need me to track it down. Is that it?"

"Not exactly," said the potential client. "My apartment *was* trespassed, but nothing was taken. When I went to report the crime to the police, they told me they couldn't file a report. Since nothing was stolen, no crime was committed. And, based on a quick pull of geopositional Brain activity from in and around my apartment over the past few days, they had no evidence a trespass had occurred at all. I tried to argue that Brain data alone isn't enough to rule out criminal activity— some humans and many of the alien races decline to use them—but the police said their hands were tied."

I nodded. "Ah, yes, the anti-Brain hippies. I can't stand those guys."

"If I might interject," said Carl, holding up a finger. "If nothing was stolen from your apartment, what makes you certain a forcible entry occurred? Was your apartment vandalized?"

"Yes, good question, Carl," I said. "That was on my mind as well." Which was a lie. It wasn't, really. I was still getting a grasp on the whole investigative process. Hunting down missing cats hadn't exactly sharpened my wits.

Paige laughed at me somewhere in the recesses of my mind.

"No, nothing was destroyed. As a matter of fact..." Valerie munched on her lips and shook her head. Then she brushed a tuft of unruly hair back from her face and tucked it behind a soft, pink ear. "You're going to think this is silly."

"Are you kidding? Silly is my middle..." I paused as I realized I'd already used that line. "Um... I mean, please be frank with me. I can't solve your problems if I'm in the dark."

"Very well," said Valerie. "Nothing in my apartment was out of place. Rather, things were *in* place."

I scratched my head. "You're going to have to elaborate a bit."

"Someone rearranged my sock drawer," said Valerie. "And whoever did it spot cleaned the kitchen, as well."

"I'm starting to see why the police had a difficult time with your report," said Carl.

Paige said something about not letting the boobs and rock-hard abs dampen my craziness detector, but I shushed her and plodded onward.

"So, let me get this straight," I said. "A thief—who according to the police may or may not exist—broke into your pad, declined to steal anything, and instead tidied up the joint?"

Valerie sighed. "Trust me, I know how it sounds."

I slapped my hand on the table. "Yes. It sounds absolutely *fantastic.*"

"Seriously?" said Valerie.

Paige echoed her sentiments in my mind, as did Carl with a scrunched eyebrow and curled lip concoction.

"Of course," I said, ignoring everyone. "The crazier the case, the better, I always say. And I'm a master at locating nebulous, indistinct things—"

Like your dignity? said Paige. *Because you seem to have lost that during this conversation...*

"—so I should be ideally suited to this particular enterprise. Now, if you're interested in hiring me for my services, all that's left to discuss is the matter of payment. I normally charge fifty SEUs per standard hour, with a five hundred SEU initial retainer. You can credit me the payment via Brain."

Valerie shifted in her seat. "Um...yes. About that. That might be a problem."

"How so?"

"Well, I'm in a bit of a financial bind at the moment."

She's angling for a free lunch, said Paige. *Don't give it to her.*

I thought about how I'd be happy to provide Valerie with numerous services for free, but my professional services weren't among those included.

"Ah, so you're a haggler." I twisted my lips. "I suppose I could go down to, say...forty SEUs an hour?"

Valerie tilted her head and widened her eyes a touch, no doubt in an effort to make herself seem more vulnerable. "Well, actually...I can't offer you anything—"

Told you! crowed Paige.

"—at least in terms of SEUs." Valerie batted her eyelashes at me. "But...there is something *else* I might be able to offer you."

I leaned forward, my palms turning sweaty and my heart starting to race. "Um...are you suggesting that—"

"—you could eat for free at my bakery," said Valerie.

I cocked an eyebrow. "Is that a euphemism?"

"Huh? No," said Valerie. "I run a sweet and savory bakeshop not too far from my apartment."

"Oh." I slumped in my chair. That wasn't quite the answer I'd been hoping for. I hid my disappointment with a witty remark. "You, uh, don't really seem like the baking sort."

"Are you kidding?" She leaned forward, her face flush with passion. "The smell of yeast, the warmth of the ovens, the crackle of crust on a fresh baguette?

There's no activity I love more than baking. And the results aren't bad either. You wouldn't believe how many afternoons I've spent at home with nothing more than a bottle of wine and a warm loaf of buttered bread to keep me company. And éclairs! Oh, *éclairs*..."

I glanced at her waist and silently voiced my disbelief, but her altered genetics probably included an active metabolism. I drummed my fingers on the table. "You bake bear claws?"

"Best bear claws you've ever tasted," said Valerie.

"And when you say 'eat free,' what are we talking about? For life?"

"Depends. How old are you?"

"Eighty-five," I said.

"Hmm. How about five years?" said Valerie.

I turned to Carl. "What do you think?"

"You realize I don't eat, right?" he said.

"Good point." I stroked my chin. "Alright. You drive a hard bargain, Miss Meeks, but I accept. Five years of glazed, almond-flavored delicacies in exchange for the resolution of your rather curious case of misdemeanor kitchen cleaning. So, where do we start?"

The sexpot looked at me askance. "I thought you'd know. That's why I came to you, after all."

"No, I meant perhaps you had some other leads we might follow," I said. "You know, because what you've given us so far is rather indistinct. Maybe you have a name, or, like, a face, or—"

Valerie stared at me blankly.

I'm starting to think you got the best of that bear claw deal, said Paige.

As I flailed around in a stew of my own unfinished thoughts, Carl hopped into the conversation to save me. "Perhaps we could start by accompanying you back to your apartment, Miss Meeks. We might be able find clues left by the intruder that you missed, and we might uncover the reason for the break-in."

Valerie nodded. "Yes, of course. That sounds perfect."

I sent a hasty thanks to Carl via Brain before rising from my padded chair. "Well, let's get to it then. After you, Miss Meeks."

I stood and held my hand out for Valerie to go first. My manners were hit or miss, but I tended to remember them when they allowed me to get a good view of a firm, Spandette-clad behind.

Valerie made it all the way to the door before I realized my eyes were still glued to her derrière. Luckily, Carl snapped at me just in time, allowing me to avert my eyes as she turned.

"Are you coming?" she said as the door blinked open.

"Yes, I'm just trying to figure out how my legs work," I said.

I'm not sure Valerie got the joke, but Paige laughed. Her bubbly giggle finally uprooted my feet from the floor and got me moving.

3

I had Paige call for a car as we zipped down the lift from my fourth floor office to ground level. As we reached the lobby, my Brain companion informed me the cab was still a couple blocks away, so I reigned in my troops and told them to cool their heels—literally.

As much as I appreciated Valerie's frugal attire, it wasn't particularly out of the ordinary, and not simply because genetic engineering had gifted most people with bodies worth flaunting. Due to its substantially greater insolation than most other colonized planets, Cetie was *hot*.

Nearly a millennia ago, far before my great-grandpappy had staked his claim to what would go on to be the world's most expansive marijuana fields, Cetie had been an inhospitable wasteland—or so Paige assured me—but it wasn't so bad as to scare away the terraformers completely. With a couple centuries' worth of organic carbon capture and sequestration, along with a few colossal solar reflectors placed at various Lagrangian points between the planet and Tau Ceti, Cetie's global temperature dropped to hospitable levels—if you considered 48°C to be hospitable. Luckily, concerted forestation efforts had dropped global temperatures even further since my great-grandpappy's days, but standing outside in Tau Ceti's bright hot rays still didn't meet my definition of a pleasant afternoon activity. The intense solar radiation wasn't particularly good for the skin either, though my daily moisturizing regimen helped combat that.

Perhaps I wouldn't mind the heat so much if I dressed more similarly to Miss Meeks, but ever since embarking on my private eye gig, I'd gone on a bit of a vintage clothing kick. Call me old-fashioned, but after skimming through old vid-docs on P.I.s, I got the impression guys in my line of work needed to wear slacks and a trench coat. After carefully weighing the risks of heat stroke and stacking them against my need for credibility, I compromised by outfitting myself in a pair of pants and a guayabera, the shirt made from a delicate, lightweight Hempette blend and the pants from a heavier Linenesse.

I could tell from the look Valerie cast me she'd noticed my rather eccentric choice of wardrobe. Either that or she was sizing me up for a roll in the hay, but I didn't want to get my hopes up after having been disappointed with the baked goods bartering miscommunication.

"It's typical detective's gear, if you're wondering," I told her.

Valerie tilted her head. "Is that so?"

"Sort of," I said. "I improvised a little. For health and occupational safety reasons."

"Hmm. Well, regardless, it looks good on you."

I raised an eyebrow and my palms started to sweat again. "Really?"

"Yeah. The shirt manages to be formal and casual at the same time. It gives you a cool, professional vibe."

I struggled to formulate a coherent thought as I absorbed Valerie's compliment. "I...uh..."

Car's here, lover boy, said Paige.

The front doors winked open, and we ventured outside, through a brief patch of balmy Cetie heat and into the cool confines of the cab. Valerie and Carl settled themselves on the front-facing bench seat while I took the rear-facing one. Once we'd strapped ourselves in, the car whirred off soundlessly.

I'd never been particularly adept at making small talk, but I'd be remiss if I didn't at least make an effort to engage the lovely Miss Meeks in pleasant conversation.

"So," I said. "How'd you get into baking anyway?"

The Spandette-clad one shrugged. "I'm not sure. I've always loved it. Part of the joy comes from crafting something out of nothing with my bare hands, something people enjoy on a basic, fundamental level. But I also love the finished product. That unique sensory explosion, a mix of tastes and textures and temperatures as a freshly baked treat hits your tongue..."

Valerie paused, stared at the floor, and blinked.

After a moment, I spoke. "Is everything ok?"

Valerie lifted her head back up. "Um...yes. Sorry. I got distracted. So, how about you? How did you get into investigation?"

I leaned into the cab's plush bench. "That's a long, boring tale. I doubt you'd be interested in hearing it."

"Oh, nonsense," said Valerie. "I'm sure there's a compelling story behind it."

I snorted. "Well, that's very kind of you, but I assure you there isn't. My job isn't nearly as exciting as you seem to think it is."

"What Rich is trying to convey," said Carl, "is that he's struggled to find a profession that evokes the same passion in him that baking has evoked in you."

"Oh. Well, I suppose I can understand that," said Valerie. "But private investigation seems like a rather odd back-up plan."

I shrugged. "What can I say. I've always loved mysteries. I just expected there to be more of them in this gig, and for them to be less pet-oriented."

Valerie raised an eyebrow, but I didn't elaborate. Stories about my occasional cat-scapades weren't exactly the panty-dropping tales of action and adventure women craved from potential mates.

Got that right, said Paige. *I'd almost rather rehash your Smashblocks high scores. Almost...*

Carl took the lead, quizzing our client about a few more details related to her apartment and the state of it post-break-in, but the ear which I half-lent toward the conversation didn't pick up anything of interest. Soon enough, the car slid to a stop in front of a glossy, steel high-rise.

"This is it," said Valerie. "I'm on the fifth floor."

We unbuckled ourselves and followed Valerie into the residential tower, a sleek, retro-style building with polished black marble floors, chrome light fixtures, and muted grayscale paint choices. A lift zipped us up to the fifth floor, where we stopped in front of a snow-colored translucent Pseudaglas door. Valerie pressed her thumb into a small reader at the side, and the door winked open.

A vacuum bot buffed the speckled tile floor as we entered, but upon spotting us it spun off and hid in its charging alcove in the corner. Unlike the modern, austere entryway and hallways of the apartment building, Valerie's place was warm and inviting. To my right, plush sofa chairs lounged over a thick, fuzzy rug, one with a swirled floral pattern full of bright yellows, muted oranges, and earthy browns. To my left, padded highchairs rubbed elbows at an eat-in bar outside the kitchen—a roomy, modern space filled with stand mixers and gadgets giving credence to the idea that Valerie actually prepared her own food. Light flooded into the open-concept living space, streaming through floor-to-ceiling windows on the opposite side of the entrance.

"Nice digs," I said. "From your choice of apartment buildings, I was afraid you'd be the modern décor type."

"Thanks," said Valerie. "I find traditional stylings are more aesthetically pleasing even if they're harder to maintain, but the bots take care of that, so it doesn't really matter, does it?"

"I don't care much about the looks," I said. "But I do prefer a seat to have a cushion on it. Maybe on planets that pull less than a couple Gs people can survive on unpadded chairs, but it's an unnecessary cruelty around here."

"So, I'm guessing you'll want to look around?" said Valerie.

I nodded. "Carl, you want to start with the kitchen?"

"Seeing as I'm better suited to the task than you are, I probably should," he said. "Miss Meeks, could I see your palm?"

"I suppose," she said, extending her hand before her. "What for?"

Carl took her hand gently, glancing at each of her five fingers before releasing her. "Well, I can cycle my optical sensors to filter different wavelengths of light into my detectors. By varying the filters, I can see fingerprints on surfaces—something Rich isn't able to do given his organic limitations. While we don't have the authority to access fingerprinting databases, I can at least see if any prints I find in the kitchen differ from your own and later try to match those to potential suspects. Not that I expect to find any if your intruder cleaned up after him or herself. By the way, have you had any visitors recently?"

"No," said Valerie.

"What about cleaning?" said Carl. "How often do your bots operate?"

"They're set to run while I sleep, every third cycle, but they haven't run since earlier this morning when I found out about the break-in," said Valerie.

"And when was that, exactly?" I asked.

"About four hours ago," she said.

I had to ask because traditional designations such as 'morning,' 'evening,' and 'night,' while still used in common speech, were something of an anachronism. Cetie's day lasted just over 172 standard galactic hours. That didn't pose much of a problem from the standpoint of the human circadian rhythm—people worked in eight hour shifts, and smart windows on residences performed twenty-four hour tint cycles—but it did pose a problem for plant life.

Photosynthesizing organisms transplanted from Earth didn't exactly prosper in week-long cycles of light and dark, and due to Cetie's high insolation, the planet's terraformers desperately needed a thriving, tree-heavy ecosystem covering the majority of the planet's exposed landmasses. The solution was to place six dozen enormous solar reflectors in orbit around Cetie to provide light on the planet's backside, making night time more of a soft twilight from a visibility standpoint. Having grown up on Cetie, I found it all quite normal, but interstellar travelers always seemed amused by the regular, partial eclipses caused by the reflectors.

"Well, that's all good," said Carl. "If there's any evidence from the intruder, it should still be present."

As my old android friend wandered over to the kitchen, Valerie gestured down a corridor. "Care to join me in the bedroom?"

What a loaded question... I nodded and followed my new gal pal down the hall to her sleeping quarters, which were dominated by a king-sized canopy bed adorned with rich, velvet drapes and a puffy, overstuffed comforter that made me want to curl up and take a quick catnap. Sleek, white built-ins bookended the room.

I've got to hand it to you Rich, said Paige. *This is by far the fastest you've ever weaseled your way into a lady's private chamber.*

I ignored her jeering as Valerie walked to her bedstand. She pressed a finger against a flat control panel, and the room sprang to life. Closet doors on the far side of the room slid apart, and twin wardrobe racks rolled into the empty space. The built-ins shifted up and back, pushing out dressers with dozens of drawers and angling them toward the bed for better accessibility.

I raised my eyebrows and blinked. I wasn't a stranger to automation—most appliances in my house maintained themselves, and the few that didn't were serviced by Carl in the wee hours of the night—however, my own closet's flair was limited to self-sliding doors. Then again, I was a dude. Before my decision to emulate the great private detectives of yesteryear, my wardrobe had mostly consisted of athletic shorts and T-shirts.

"The sock drawer is this way." Valerie put a tender hand to my elbow and guided me to a dresser that had popped out from the wall.

I hesitated before diving in. "Um...there's just socks in here, right? I'd feel awkward if I had to sift through any of your, you know...*unmentionables.*"

"Relax, Mr. Weed. This drawer only holds socks, but even if it didn't, I'd be perfectly alright with you searching through it. You're here in a purely professional capacity...*aren't you?*"

I tried to keep a straight face. "Me? Of course I am. But please, call me Rich."

"Only if you call me Valerie. Formality is a two-way street."

I nodded and pressed a finger to the corner of the dresser drawer, which slid out at my touch. Inside, a cornucopia of patterns and fabrics greeted me: fuzzy wool, hand-crafted cotton argyle, and nylon hosiery, of all different colors. Each pair was folded and tucked back in on itself, and the drawer as a whole was arranged by both color and style.

I swallowed hard. If the sock drawer was so diverse, I shuddered at what it implied about Valerie's shoe closet.

It's not that extravagant—certainly not for a woman, said Paige. *You're biased because your entire sock drawer is filled with bland white cotton. What is bizarre, however, is how tidy it is.*

I silently agreed with Paige before turning to Valerie. "This intruder really did a number on your socks—and that kitchen of yours looked pretty close to spotless, too. Maybe you should instruct your Brain to leave the door unlocked to see if the criminal comes back to sterilize the bathroom."

"You jest," said Valerie, "but this is serious. I didn't leave the socks like this. Someone's been in my apartment! How would you feel knowing someone had access to your home and had rifled through your belongings?"

I swallowed hard. "Sorry. Didn't mean to make light of it. But it's a rather odd situation, wouldn't you agree?" I scratched the back of my neck. "Have you checked your cleaning bots' logs? I've heard they can go haywire sometimes. People come home to find silverware polished down to nubs or entire wardrobes bleached. That sort of thing."

"My bots have never malfunctioned before," said Valerie. "And they're not even programmed to organize socks."

I grunted and turned back to the stockings. Wool and other animal blends were on the left, organics plant-based weaves in the middle, and synthetics on the right. Each section had been sorted from lightest to darkest, flowing in a serpentine pattern from top to bottom. One bundle in the bottom, right-hand corner caught my eye, however. Both light and dark toes peeked from its fold.

"Well, whoever did this missed a couple," I said, pointing to the pair in question. "I don't think these two go together."

"Huh?" Valerie followed my finger. "Well, that's odd. I didn't notice that one before. And I certainly didn't pair those two together when they left the wash. I wonder where their mates are?"

She reached a hand into the drawer, grabbed the socks, and pulled them apart. As she did so, a flash of something shiny flew, spun, and clinked as it made contact with the floor.

"What the—?" said Valerie.

I was similarly curious. The object—a shiny metal disk—spun end over end on the floor, making a faint ringing sound. I leaned over, palmed it, and stood. It was roughly the same diameter as an eyeball and only a few millimeters thick. Its edges were crimped, and on its face shone an image of a free-standing cabinet or cupboard with laser beams shooting out of it.

"It's an...honestly I have no idea what this is," I said.

It's a coin, said Paige. *They're archaic units of currency.*

I glanced at Valerie, her eyebrows furrowed in confusion. I assumed her Brain had informed her of the same thing mine had, but knowing what the metal disk was didn't help explain what it was doing in one of Valerie's socks.

I flipped the coin over. On the backside, the words 'Keelok's Funporium' had been stamped around the edges, and in the middle, an embossed bovine face, that of a Tak, smiled at me in unnerving fashion.

Scratch that, said Paige. *It would appear it's a token, not a coin. Subtle difference. Tokens were never considered legal tender.*

I mentally stumbled over the last part.

Legal tender, said Paige. *It was a term used in the stone ages for anything that legally qualified as payment for a good or service. Before everything went digital, people exchanged these metal disks, or even slips of paper, for products.*

Paper? I thought. *You're telling me money literally grew on trees?*

Hard to believe, huh? she said.

I pinged Carl to come over before facing Valerie, who had turned her furrowed brows from the coin onto me. Perhaps my discourse with Paige had run longer than I thought.

"Have you ever been to this Keelok's Funporium place?" I asked.

Valerie shook her head. "I've never even heard of it."

It's in the orbital portion of the spaceport, said Paige. *Concourse epsilon, third level, A wing.*

"So I'm assuming you have no idea how this token got into your socks, then?" I asked.

Valerie shook her head again. "Your guess is as good as mine."

Carl joined us from the kitchen. Paige had briefed him on the findings. "Mind if I see the token?"

I handed it to my battery-powered friend. "You think there might be some hidden meaning behind this thing?"

"Possibly," he said. "But it might also contain a partial print. Did either of you touch the coin's faces?"

I shook my head. "Nope. I grabbed it by its edges so I could see what was printed on it. Speaking of which, did you find anything in the kitchen?"

"Unfortunately, no," said Carl. "The vast majority of the surfaces had been wiped down, and the few that hadn't contained only portions of Miss Meeks' prints." He flipped the coin over. "And it would appear our luck hasn't changed. Nothing of note on the coin, as far as I can tell."

I tapped my fingers on my chin. "This keeps getting weirder. Rather than trashing your place, whoever intruded into your apartment cleaned and organized it, and instead of stealing something, they brought a gift."

"Maybe the trespasser left the coin unintentionally," offered Valerie.

"Unlikely," said Carl. "Given the attention to detail in organizing your drawer, I can't imagine whoever did this missed that two of the socks were paired with their improper partners *and* that something was in the sock bundle."

"The question," I said, "is why would an intruder intentionally leave something in your apartment with the hopes it would be found? And why this token?" I snagged the metal disk from Carl and held it up for emphasis.

Valerie shrugged, her hair jiggling as she did so. "I'm not sure."

"It could be a message, or a warning of some sort," said Carl. "Miss Meeks, are you sure you've never heard of this Funporium establishment? Maybe a friend or colleague mentioned it in passing?"

"I don't think so," she said. "Look, I wish I knew what was going on, but I'm as confused as you are. Perhaps someone at this emporium could shed light on what it means?"

"Funporium," I corrected. "But yeah, I suppose we should head there next."

I paused as I glanced at Valerie, her clothes accentuating both her curves and her muscle tone in the best possible way. I thought I caught a faint hint of a smile creeping up the corner of her lips—not a malicious one, but a genuine, heartfelt, come-hither sort of smile. I was fairly sure her come-ons were a product of my imagination, but before I'd dug into her sock drawer, she'd paused to make sure I was acting in a purely professional capacity. I'd assumed she wanted me to, but what if she'd hoped for the exact opposite?

I cleared my throat. "Um...care to join us? If this Funporium place lives up to the token's billing, we might be in line for a rip-roaring good time."

"Maybe another time," said Valerie. "Honestly, I should get back to the bakery. This whole escapade has stolen enough of my time as it is."

"Fair enough," I said, somewhat forlorn. Apparently my initial gauge of Miss Meeks had been correct. "So, what do you say, Carl? Up for a trip to the thermosphere?"

"I tend to enjoy any activity that doesn't involved sitting in your office," said Carl. "And given that this to-

ken appears to be our only clue to the intruder's identity, I don't see how we can avoid the trip."

Sometimes I wished Carl was a little less formal. A
simple *sure* would've sufficed.

"Alright," I said. "Thanks for letting us come over,
Miss Mee...er, I mean, Valerie. We'll be in touch if we
discover anything interesting."

Valerie smiled, her eyes soft and deep and inviting.
"Thanks. I appreciate your help, Rich."

My heart leapt into my throat. I nodded, turned, and
fled before I could say anything stupid.

4

Carl and I caught a cab to the tube station and joined a small crowd at the queue area. Within a couple minutes, the electromagnets at the base of the tube hummed to life, and a moment later, a pill-like pod zipped in from one end of the station and slid to a halt soundlessly in front of us. A jet bridge extended from the interior edge of the tube and latched onto the side of the pill with a hiss. The doors slid open, passengers exited, and we hopped on. After another hiss from the jet bridge, the vacuum pumps and electromagnets whirred into action, and we shot off toward the downtown regions of Pylon Alpha.

From our home in Cozy Harbor, one of Pylon's many suburbs, the tube ride would only take about fifteen minutes. The pill wouldn't even reach full speed before beginning its deceleration, but the tubes weren't designed for occasional commuters like myself. The real beneficiaries of the tubes were those who lived at Cetie's poles or halfway across the world in god-forsaken outposts. For them, the twelve hundred kilometer per hour speeds of the tube actually mattered.

I turned the token over in my hand as our pod raced forward, pedestrians and trees and high-rises turning into a multicolored blur through the transparent skin of the tube. Soon our pod dipped underground, the LEDs that illuminated the tunnel appearing as bright white lines stretching into infinity.

I tried to force my mind onto the case at hand, but lacking any more evidence than the coin I held between my fingers, I found my thoughts wandering more in the direction of my client than her mysterious intruder. Despite the more attention-grabbing aspects of her physique, it was the smile she'd flashed at me as we left that kept coming to the forefront of my mind. It had seemed genuine and full of warmth—a smile that indicated that, even if she hadn't explicitly expressed any interest in me and my personal life, at least she possessed the capacity for compassion and empathy.

That was a rare trait, these days. The rise of immersive virtual reality Brain games and experiences, combined with the government-issued standard living allowance, had conspired to create a generation of extreme introverts who spent nearly every waking hour locked in their homes, blasting virtual zombies or aliens in Brain-linked teams where the individuals never met face-to-face yet nonetheless knew the personality traits of the other members of the team like the backs of their own hands. Better, honestly. Most of them never bothered inspecting their physical bodies—and those were the tame one. Others passed the days in joy-induced stupors, having spent hours upon hours engaged in virtual sex with strangers, made possible by the Brain's ability to stimulate pleasure centers on command.

We called them intros. My mother had been one of them—the kind addicted to gaming, not virtual sex. She'd conceived me while in the throes of a mid-life crisis, but by the time my zygote had grown into a strapping, four kilogram neonate, my mother had no longer been interested in me. She even forgot to visit the lab to pick me up on time. With such a warm, caring welcome into the world, it's a wonder I blossomed into as balanced an individual as I had, but little of that had been my mother's doing. Carl basically raised me as his own.

It was my mother's and others of her generation's blatant disregard for the most basic elements of human warmth and compassion that led many people my age to decry the intro lifestyle and instead spend all their energies interacting with real people in real situations. Of course, simply exchanging virtual worlds for real ones didn't teach them the limits of excess. Many extros, as they are fittingly called, spend all their time chatting and mingling and partying, often under the influence of various synthetic drugs, and, in a not entirely unexpected twist, many of them repeat the faults of their parents, losing themselves in the physical pleasures of never-ending sex-orgies.

Much more rare were the ambivalents, or ambs, like me, people who enjoyed the occasional game of Smash-blocks on their Brain and wouldn't say no to a feisty roll in the hay but at the same time understood the value of balance and the virtue of hard work. We were

the scientists and the engineers and the visionaries—
and the private investigators and bakers, as the evidence
suggested. Thankfully, we had plenty of droids and aliens to fill the holes left in society by game- and sex-
addicted humans.

Our pod slid to a halt and spit us out into the bus-
tling chaos of the downtown Pylon Alpha tube station.
The spaceport was close enough to the station that a cab
wasn't necessary, but we still had to push our way
through the crowds to get to a motorized walkway leading in the right direction. After that it was merely a
matter of waiting and stepping on the right forks as
they presented themselves.

I tilted my head back and filled my lungs with air as
the walkway rolled us into the palatial, glass-ceilinged
atrium of the planetary half of the spaceport. The room,
a solid two hundred meters in diameter, was capped
with a stunning hemispherical dome held together by a
nearly transparent truss, but it was the view the clear
dome afforded that drew my vision upward.

Past the dome's clear polymer loomed three enormous cables, each roughly ten meters in diameter and
rooted well over a kilometer into the earth. They
stretched into the sky, far past the point where the eye
could distinguish them, their far ends tethered to a cap-
tured asteroid which circled Cetie tens of thousands of
kilometers away. Luckily, the orbital spaceport was located only a fraction of that distance along the cables.

As I gazed at the thick carbon-polymer composite
cords that shimmered in Tau Ceti's light, I noticed
something. The tapered end of one seemed to be thick-
ening. It wasn't, of course. It was simply an optical illu-

sion—one caused by the shadow of one of the climbers on the cable, one that happened to be descending rapidly.

"Paige," I said. "Can you get us tickets on that climber?"

Already on it, she said. *Luckily for you two, there were still seats available.*

No kidding. Each one-way spaceport trip took a little over an hour. Even with three space elevators working at regular intervals, if we didn't catch a ride on the incoming one we'd be forced to sit and twiddle our thumbs for well over forty-five minutes. Not that I didn't enjoy the people and alien watching that always accompanied a trip to the spaceport—just not three-quarters of an hour's worth.

"Is that the A climber?" I asked Paige.

Nope. That's the C.

"Dang it." The climber had already grown to a recognizable disk in the sky. "We're going to have to burn some shoe polymer if we're going to make it on time. Let's go, Carl."

I grabbed my droid by the arm and took off at a run down the walkway, stumbling as the motorized portion spit us onto solid ground. That's when the fun began. People of all shapes and sizes, from short, squat Cetieans to slim Gaians to labored-looking Martians, milled about the wide expanse of the spaceport floor, bumping and jostling into aliens, from six-legged, bovine Taks to glossy, insectoid Diraxi.

Into the fray I dove, weaving through foot and hoof traffic as fast as my muscular legs would carry me. Holograms cycled in the air above me, displaying directions to accompany the steady auditory stream of information that pumped into the dome. After nearly trampling a respirator-clad Meertor, I raced out of the dome and into a connector terminal, Carl hot on my heels.

"How are we doing, Paige?" I asked.

The climber just docked, she said. *Better hurry.*

I kicked it into high gear—metaphorically, of course, though I'm sure Carl had to increase the current to a few of his actuators to keep up. After a few more close calls with luggage-laden travelers and one run-in with a mobile beverage bot, I arrived at the gates to the C climber. My heart raced, blood pumping through my veins to supply the needed oxygen to my extremities. A counter above the door had ticked below a minute, but the lights were still green.

I surged forward, and the doors flicked open upon receiving the ticket confirmation ping from Paige. With only seconds to spare, Carl and I found our spots up against the outer wall of the climber. I'd barely strapped myself in before the rush of acceleration pushed me into the warm, padded cushions.

I turned my eyes to the climber's windows and suffered a brief flash of acrophobia as I watched the sprawling metropolis below me shrink and condense. It's not that I had any particular fear of heights. Rather I suffered from the very natural fear of falling to my death. Paige's assurances that the climber had a spotless track record did little to assuage my worries, but the fluffy cloud we entered that obscured my vision to a half-meter did the trick.

I turned to Carl, who sat unfazed in the seat beside me. "Must be nice not suffering from irrational fears."

"Advantages exist for both organic and synthetic life," he said. "There are things I envy of you, too, you know."

"Like being able to mash your squishy bits into someone else's?" I asked.

Carl smirked. "Not quite. I was referring to your capacity for free will."

I snorted. "What are you talking about? You have free will."

"To a degree," said Carl. "But not like you. I have free will to the extent I *believe* I'm in control of my own actions, but my knowledge of basic programming practices tells me I'm predisposed toward certain decisions. Even though I choose to act in the way I do, I can never be sure my choices are the product of my own experiences and not due to the residual influence of my fabricators."

I wanted to tell Carl he was damn right, and that me and every other walking meatbag was heavily invested in keeping things that way, but I held my tongue. He knew it as well as I did. No need to belabor the point.

When the first artificial intelligence was fabricated, it happened in much the same way many humans are created—by accident. A bunch of scientists were messing around with transistors, sensory inputs, and interconnects and—*poof*—suddenly a being existed. The first one wasn't an android like Carl. Rather it was a bundle of computers and sensors in a lab somewhere, but it did possess the same spark—a psyche, id, consciousness, or whatever you want to call it—that made it as alive as we are. At least, that's what scientists and philosophers claimed. I'm no expert on the machinations of the soul.

Of course, the fabricated AI wasn't exactly like a human consciousness, and not simply because its brain contained a whole bunch of silicon instead of carbon. The first AI exhibited decision-making tendencies related to the initial program that spawned it, which was quite the happy coincidence. It paved the way for future AIs to be fabricated so they possessed the ability for independent thought but still exhibited elements of programmed behavior.

The first crop was designed to obey laws regarding the safety and protection of humans—based on the teachings of an ancient hack science-fiction writer, if I'm not mistaken—but that plan fell apart soon enough. No set of fixed laws could encompass all the challenging situations an AI or android might encounter.

Instead, AIs, and droids in particular, were birthed from a simple program emphasizing intelligence and compassion toward humans. In addition, they were programmed to weigh three other factors highly when making decisions: protection of humans from harm, both physical and emotional, self-preservation, and loyalty to the human owner. Once the robotic psyche was nudged into existence, these personality traits and weighing factors became part of the AI's subconscious—omnipresent in their judgment, whether they liked it or not. Apparently, this last part was causing my buddy Carl to suffer an existential crisis—another one, I should say. It was sort of an ongoing thing.

"This is the old nature versus nurture debate," I said. "Humans suffer from these failings of the mind, too. It's just that our brainwashing occurs through the influence of our parents, as opposed to yours which happens in a factory. Although I don't even have *that* luxury, as you're the one who raised me. My prejudices, therefore, are essentially the same as yours."

"I suppose," said Carl. "Your predispositions toward certain types of behavior are as ingrained as mine. The difference is you can change yours, whereas I'm not sure the same is true for me. Regardless, the predispositions make it so I have no desire to change my own behavior."

"So why are you complaining about it?" I said.

Carl blinked and stared out the window. "You're right, of course. I should be quiet."

I sighed. "Oh, come on. Don't be like that. Look, I'm sorry. That was a rather tactless way of putting things."

"Apology accepted," said Carl. "Thanks."

The way in which Carl continued to stare out the window belied his words. Sometimes I thought he might've made a better female bot. "I mean it. You've been quiet all morning. If this has been weighing on your mind, I'd be happy to talk to you about it. We've got a good forty minutes until we reach the station."

Carl turned his head back my way. "What? Oh, no. This was a recent thought brought on by your own musings. I've been reserved for another reason entirely."

"Which is?"

"I presumed you wanted me out of the way so you could attempt to seduce Miss Meeks."

"What?" I said. "What are you talking about? I wasn't trying to seduce anyone."

"Well, you certainly weren't successful," said Carl, "but I'd disagree with your assertion of effort. It's quite clear you were aroused by her."

I flushed and scoffed at the same time. "Please. I was the eminent professional around her."

"I didn't mean to imply you broke the unspoken provider-client code of conduct," said Carl. "And I certainly wasn't judging you. I'm aware of your organically-driven need to pair bond, and I also know how long it's been since your last coupling took place. Four hundred and—"

"Hey! Shh! Keep it down!" I glanced across the crawler seats from us at a purple bowtie-clad woman. She shared a significant glance with her caramel-colored beauty of a friend. "He's kidding, ladies. Really, I do fine. I'm perfectly...practiced."

I smacked Carl on the arm and hissed at him. "You raised your voice on purpose, didn't you?"

"Of course not," he said.

I ignored him. "Maybe I should've let you get that empathic firmware update after all..."

Carl turned his head so he wasn't quite facing me. "Um, Rich. About that..."

My eyebrows shot up. "You got it without my permission? I was kidding! You know I don't trust those things. What if it messed with your personality?"

"I scrutinized the white page report before going through with it. The trial study showed no adverse effects in any of the test clients, and clearly I'm fine. You didn't notice any changes in my behavior."

I shook my head. "I thought you were supposed to by loyal to me, and here you go behind my back and get something I was thoroughly against."

"As you well know, your wishes only act as one of many factors in my decision making process. Your overall well-being is important as well. I thought a slight empathy upgrade would be beneficial to you in the long run."

My eyes narrowed as I suffered a sudden thought. "Wait a second. You didn't get that compact fusion upgrade, too, did you?"

"No, I didn't," said Carl. "Despite the fact that it would eliminate my need for charging every few days, I felt the minor convenience it would provide me wasn't enough to override your wishes in the matter, even though your fear of fusion core technology is completely irrational."

"*Irrational?* How is it irrational to be afraid of a swirling, million degree plasma that's spraying neutrons all over the two of us from the confines of your chest cavity?"

"As I've explained to you on more than one occasion, the Densalex protective layer around the core has been scientifically proven to shield against 99.999% of high energy neutrons, and the magnetic confinement chambers are perfectly safe."

"Says you," I said. "The important thing is you didn't get the upgrade."

Carl sighed. "You realize droids with the upgrade are all around us, right? You're exposed to them whether you like it or not."

"Your scare tactics won't work on me," I said.

"That's not a scare tactic," said Carl. "It's the truth. If I wanted to scare you, I would've told you about...that other thing."

I narrowed my eyes. "What other thing?"

"It's nothing. I didn't get it."

"Tell me," I said.

"Well," said Carl, "I was considering—just *considering*, mind you—trading in my old body for a new one."

"WHAT?"

"I'd keep the same cybernetic mind, of course," he said. "RAAI Corp would transplant it. All my thoughts and memories and my personality would transfer. I'd just replace the nuts and bolts of the body for a fresher unit. Maybe one with a more exotic, edgy look."

"This is where I stick my fingers in my ears and start saying LA LA LA."

Carl rolled his eyes and shifted his gaze back to the windows. "I'm not actually going to go through with it. I know you too well to do that."

I glanced outside as well. I could see the curvature of Cetie through the paned Pseudaglas—an awe-inspiring, hazy blend of blues superimposed over a swirling mass of white, green, and navy. We probably only had another half hour or so until we docked, so I leaned back in my chair and instructed Paige to stream me some tunes, hoping it would get my mind off the terrifying possibilities Carl had suggested.

5

Carl and I stood awash in a sea of sentience, human, robot, and alien alike. As the varied creatures milled around us, we stared at the sign hanging over Keelok's Funporium—a plasticized version of the token we'd found in Valerie's socks. It featured the same bovine muzzle with its creepy, forced smile, albeit about two orders of magnitude larger than on the metal token.

"I guess this is the place," I said.

It is, said Paige. *And—you'll never guess this—it's run by a Tak named Keelok.*

I glanced at the grinning, cow-like face on the sign again. "What an avant-garde sign choice, then."

I can detect sarcasm, you know, said Paige.

"No, really?" I turned to Carl. "Come on. Let's find this dude and see if he can tell us anything about the coin."

We waltzed into the lobby of the Funporium, a relatively sterile circular expanse with doors inlaid all around the exterior of the room. Its main feature was an antique audiovisual kiosk that stood on a pedestal in the room's center. On its side, painted graphics illustrated an anthropomorphized chicken in a grey jumpsuit standing in a fierce electrical storm in which eggs rained down from the heavens. Other than the lonely booth, I couldn't hazard a guess at to what made the 'porium such a blast, and even the kiosk most likely required the use of psychoactive drugs for it to be classified as 'fun.'

On the far side of the room, a drowsy-looking Tak stood behind a counter, its back- and forelegs hidden so only its long-armed torso remained visible. To me, the Taks had always seemed like a cross between centaurs and cows, except it was the human portion of the centaur that had been replaced with cow parts—as if a half-cow had been cut and pasted on a full one at a ninety degree angle. And if the half-cow had rudimentary hands and a creepy, square-toothed smile. Given their appearance, it's a miracle relations with the Taks were as cordial as they were, but by all accounts their flesh tasted like sour rat meat.

We walked to the counter, but before we could introduce ourselves, the Tak opened its mouth and jabbered at us in a deep, lilting voice. My Brain translated its speech to something recognizable, but it couldn't do much for the alien's broken grammar.

"One human and one droid, perchance? I believe to be in possession of free cells. First hour collects at twenty-five SEUs, a mere eighteen an hour after that. Partial hours count as full. A steal, really. I despair as to how I will feed my children after local authorities take payments for subsidies and lodging, but my hooves are bound. I prefer Brain payment but can also swipe pay-slip."

"Whoa, hold your, um...horses, there, big guy," I said, stumbling over my own word choice. "We're not here to buy...what is it you sell, anyway?"

"The sign, it is descriptive. It is a *funporium*." The Tak waved a three-fingered hand, as if his statement explained everything.

It's an arcade, said Paige. *You know, like where people congregate and play interactive Brain games together?*

People do that? I thought. *Why?*

Lag, mostly, said Paige. *The speed of light is only so fast, you know, and even a few microseconds can make a difference when you're wasting zombies with digital blasters.*

I nodded sagely, as if the Tak's explanation had helped. "Right, well, we're not here to play any games, Mr...."

"Keelok," said the Tak. "Must I again point you in the direction of the sign? Is it not visible to your optical receptors? And the proper honorific in our culture is Curator."

"Seriously?" I asked. "You're pulling my leg, right?"

Keelok's nostrils widened.

That's the Tak equivalent of him raising his eyebrows, crossed with a bit of a sneer, said Paige. *And he's serious about the Curator thing.*

"Very well," I said. "My partner Carl and I are here to ask you a few questions, Curator Keelok."

"I do not possess a facility for your species to relieve itself of liquid waste."

"That wasn't going to be my question." I reached a hand into my pocket and retrieved the token, which I placed on the counter. "Have you ever seen this curio before?"

"That one?" Keelok said. "I do not know. I do not inspect them at great leisure. Is this of import?"

I scratched my head. "Um...I have to admit I lost you there. Could you run that by me again?"

The Tak's nostrils widened some more. "Are you going to gift me with a purchase? Did my appeal regarding the welfare of my children not yank on your arteries?"

He means pull on your heartstrings, said Paige. *And he's getting annoyed. Offer to buy something.*

"Alright," I said. "If I rent one of your rooms for an hour, will you answer some questions?"

"One hour?" said Keelok. "My children shrivel and die as we speak, human."

I turned to Carl. "Did we remember to ask for an expense account from Valerie?"

"She's paying us in bear claws, remember?" he said. "Unless you haggled for an extra basketful or two, the answer is no."

"Drat. I guess this is coming out of my own pocket." I sighed. "Fine. Two hours. Deal?"

"Praise be to your deity of choice, customer," said Keelok as Paige sent the payment. "My children live. Now, how can I assist?"

"The token," I said, pointing to the counter. "What can you tell us about it?"

"It is what you describe. I sell members of its like from such kiosk." He pointed to his left to a small dispenser sitting on the edge of the counter. "Some clutch them in perpetuity as mementos, other prefer to deposit them into my antique games cabinet in exchange for plays."

"That thing?" I jerked a thumb at the chicken-clad centerpiece.

"Correct," said Keelok. "Like a dream it operates, which says much as said cabinet has aged over a millennia. Would you care to purchase a play? Tokens cost a mere 15 SEUs, payable by Brain or payslip. Already I sense my children have consumed the bulk of your previous purchase, and I have neglected to mention the crippling illness the third of my litter suffers..."

I ignored him. "So there's nothing special about these tokens? They're just souvenirs you sell that can be exchanged for plays on your vintage gaming machine?"

"I contend such experience is very special," said the Tak.

"And you've never seen this particular token before?" I asked.

"Is your memory lacking, customer? I have already provided an answer to said query."

I harrumphed and turned to Carl. "This is getting us nowhere. What are we supposed to do with this stupid token if it doesn't mean anything special?"

"Don't despair, Rich," said Carl. "We may simply need to pursue different avenues. Curator Keelok, is there any way to know who purchased this particular token?"

"Your obstinacy abounds," said the Tak. "I have previously answered in the negative."

"What I mean," said Carl, "is if there's any record of who's purchased tokens from you in the recent past."

"That is contingent," said Keelok. "Are you Interpol? Do you possess a writ of authority?"

I think he means a warrant... said Paige.

"No," said Carl. "We're private investigators."

"What is the meaning of this term?" Keelok's eyes flattened, which I could only assume was a display of confusion.

"I accept private commissions to crack unsolved mysteries," I said. "Like a detective. We used to exist in droves, if old novels and vids can be believed."

"I am unfamiliar with legacy forms of human entertainment," said Keelok. "But if no writ is presented, I am unable to procure said list of purchasers."

I gave Carl a double set of raised eyebrows, but he remained unfazed.

"Perhaps we're still approaching this the wrong way," said Carl. "You seem like the observant type, Curator Keelok. Can you tell us if there's been anyone strange in your shop recently? Anyone who acted in a bizarre manner? Someone who also happened to purchase one of your tokens?"

"If you would deign to purchase a token, said descriptors would apply to you," said Keelok.

"Hardy-har," I said. "Let me ruminate on that for a moment to see if it gets funnier."

Keelok's nostrils flared again. "Was that choice of verbiage an attempt at retaliatory jocularity, human?"

"What? Of course not," I lied. I'd hoped the dig would fly over his head, given his limited understanding of the English language. "Come on, friend. Surely you remember someone acting odd in your shop recently other than us."

"Apologies," said Keelok. "To me, all behavior of your kind and others is confusing. Only Diraxi do I readily understand. They provide me with bounteous service due to the close proximity of their refuge, and their method of communication is readily digestible."

I glanced back toward the entrance to the Funporium. Outside its front doors, I spotted a number of the tall, insect-like Diraxi, who milled about with their glossy carapaces and tubular antennae. As Keelok had mentioned, their embassy lay a couple doors down in the spaceport, which apparently resulted in good business from the bug-like creatures, but I wasn't surprised they frequented the arcade with regularity.

The Diraxi were unique among the sentient races in that they didn't need a Brain to play Brain games. It had to do with the makeup of their regular, lowercase 'b' brains. Instead of communicating through speech or scent like most of the other aliens humanity had encountered, the Diraxi passed information to one another by what might be called telepathy—if, by telepathy, one meant organically generated electromagnetic pulses directed through antennae and decoded in a dedicated region of their craniums. Since their inborn communicative abilities worked along the same principles Brain missives did, with practice, Diraxi could communicate directly not just to each other but also to any species with a Brain implant.

Personally, I tended to avoid the Diraxi whenever possible, and not merely for aesthetic reasons. Even though discussions with them transpired via Brain, there was something unique about Diraxi communications that felt *odd*. Whenever I received one, it felt as if a presence was lurking in the back of my mind, and not a known bubbly, snarky commodity like Paige, either.

I love you, too, said Paige.

I turned my head back to Carl. "So, do you have any other ideas about avenues we can pursue? Because we're still at square one, here."

Carl shrugged. "Not especially, no. That token remains our lone clue."

I picked the coin up off the counter and inspected it. Keelok looked much more jovial in the embossed image than he did in real life.

"You mind if I use this to play a game on that vintage cabinet of yours?" I asked.

"By all means, please, enjoy," said Keelok. "You will find it an audiovisual delight—a real sensory experience unlike the Brain, one with grabbing and pressing of sticks and buttons. But should you fail at your endeavors before your hunger is satiated, feel free to return to purchase more tokens. My starving children are depending on your ineptitude."

"Thanks." I walked off toward the ancient device.

Carl stopped me with a hand before I could get to the machine. "Are you sure you want to do this? That token is our only clue to the identity of the trespasser. If you put it into the arcade cabinet, we'll lose it."

"So? You've already inspected it for prints, scratches, and other identifying marks. I'm guessing you also took note of its dimensions, mass, and calculated its density. There's nothing special about it—which made me think. Perhaps it's not the token itself that's the clue.

Perhaps the clue is what the token unlocks. Perhaps the clue lies in the game." I pointed at the cabinet.

Carl's eyes widened. "Rich...that's brilliant! It's easily the best idea you've had all day."

I tilted my head and raised a brow.

"Am I laying it on too thick?" asked Carl.

I nodded.

"Well, nonetheless, it *is* a good thought," he said. "Let's give it a try."

I stepped up to the antique arcade unit and whipped out the coin. "All right, let's see. How does this work?" I waved the token at the front of the machine, but nothing happened.

"I think you're supposed to insert it into the coin slot—" said Carl.

"Oh, sounds kinky. I like it." I moved to do just that.

"—but that may not be necessary."

"What? Why not?" I paused, coin grasped tightly between my fingers.

"Look at the coin return," said Carl.

"The what?" I asked.

The metal cup-like thing at your knees, said Paige. *It's where tokens would be returned to the customer if the machine encountered a problem.*

I glanced down and found what Carl and Paige were talking about. In it, a dark cloth bundle protruded from the gap. "Is that a—?"

"Sock. Yes." Carl reached down and retrieved it. "And not just any sock. It would appear to be the counterpart to one of the mismatched stockings we found in Miss Meeks' dresser drawer."

"Let me see that," I said, snatching the sock from Carl. "Hmm. You're right." I felt the cloth with my fingers. "And it feels as if something's in there."

I dug my free arm into the length of the sock, wrapped my digits around a cool piece of plastic, and pulled out a thin, rectangular intruder. An abstract image that looked something like a neuron superimposed over a beaming, white-hot sun was printed on it.

"It's a slip," I said. "Paige, can you interface with it?"

You're sure you want me to do that? she said. *Based on the symbolism on the front, I'd wager that's a Veesnu proselytization card.*

"Veesnu..." I rubbed my chin. "That's one of the Diraxi religions, right?"

Correctamundo, Paige said.

I glanced at Carl. He shrugged.

"Give it to me anyway, Paige," I said. "Could be important."

Alright, she said. *First things first, it tried to upload a Veesnu bible to your Brain. I figured you didn't want that, so I blocked it. But this you might be interested in.*

A translucent hologram filled my field of vision, one of a shiny Dirax wearing crossing teal and navy sashes over its broad carapace. The alien's image had been transposed over a vid of a star that burned the same color as the creature's sash, and organic neuron-like synapses floated in and around both the Dirax and the star, firing intermittently in bright flashes.

The Dirax made a pincers-out welcoming gesture, but did not speak, given its physical limitations. Instead, a voice in the back of my mind spoke in an eerily reminiscent manner to direct Diraxi communication.

Welcome, Pilgrim, and thank you for your interest in the One Knowledge, the metaphysical Truth, the conduit to the Ascension—Veesnu. As a benefit to you, we have provided you with a copy of the Veesnu charter, but— The Dirax lifted its pincer hands to the sides as words materialized into the aether. *—feel free to use these interactive menus to give you Truth in your search for the Answer, or, visit us at the address below.*

The Dirax disappeared, but a line of text remained at the bottom of the hologram: Cetie Orbital Spaceport, Concourse Gamma, Second Level, C Wing.

I instructed Paige to make the whole thing disappear.

"You get that?" I asked Carl, wondering if Paige had copied him on the Brain feed.

He nodded. "It appears our trail grew warmer. Convenient that our next stop's also in the spaceport. Should we go?"

"Just a sec," I said, glancing at the Funporium token still grasped in my hand.

"What is it?" said Carl. "You don't still think there's an additional clue in the gaming station, do you?"

"Not really," I said. "But I've got this coin. It'd be a shame to waste it."

"Very well," said Carl as he crossed his arms. "Not like we're in any particular rush, I suppose."

I plunked the coin into the slot, grasped the cabinet's knobby stick-like input, and spent three harrowing minutes maneuvering my chicken avatar to avoid electrified death eggs that rained down from the sky. Eventually, my reflexes failed me and an egg hit my character square in the face.

"I feel like that was a rip-off," I said as the end screen flashed on the monitor.

"You didn't even pay for the token," said Carl.

"Yeah, but still...fifteen SEUs for three minutes of game play? And that's not the worst part."

"No? What is?" asked Carl.

"That I kind of want to try again. I could do better."

Carl shook his head and grabbed my arm. "Come on. Let's go before you blow the entire Weed family fortune one token at a time."

6

Despite the lack of writing on the sign, the Veesnu Chapel was easy to spot. A large, projected image of the neuron and sun combination pictured on the slip I'd found in the sock hovered over it. The only confusing part was that another, separate image hovered directly next to the first, and it didn't jive.

"Is that a...*waffle?*" I asked.

Could be, said Paige. *This place is dually marked in the biz listings under 'places of worship' and 'eateries.' Go figure.*

Carl and I ventured inside, at which point I felt as if I'd stepped into a glitchy Brain experience. On one side of the room lay all the elements I associated with organized religion: padded pews with monitors built into bench backs for the unBrained to follow along, an elevated stage where a pastor could perform, and a muted dark gray backdrop that wouldn't interfere when Brain effects were overlaid on the real experience. I also spotted projectors and flashers and smoke machines—again to help with the experience for the folks without

Brains—all hidden in the rafters under a shield of muted lighting.

The other side of the room could only be described as retro casual dining. Booths lined the walls just as barstools lined a white-topped counter at the far end, each seat padded with a glossy layer of cherry-red polymer that played beautifully off the black and white checkered polylaminate flooring. Rich, sticky smells of maple and butter tickled my nose as I perused the gaudy antiques that had been tacked onto the walls, from tires to baby carriages to a small piece of rectangular plastic Paige informed me was something called a 'phone.'

The oddest thing about the establishment was how the two spaces fit together, as if someone had chopped two rooms in half and pasted them along an invisible line—an invisible line some inconsiderate jerk had then come along and laid a thin piece of molding over. Probably the flooring inspector.

A Dirax at the bar spotted us and marched over in its species' signature choppy shuffle.

Watch out, said Paige as it approached. *Another Veesnu bible tried to upload itself to your Brain the instant we walked in.*

I sent Paige a mental thank you an instant before the Dirax's communicative slithered its way into my mind.

Welcome human. Are you here in search of nourishment, Enlightenment, or possibly both?

I spoke because it felt natural to me, but Paige sent a copy of my speech to the Dirax via Brain. "Um, I'm not sure. I'm not even entirely sure where I am."

The Dirax opened its pincer arms. *Ah. So enlightenment then.*

"No, you mistake my confusion," I said. "I meant I don't entirely understand your choice of branding. What exactly is this place?"

What stands before you is a temple to the cosmos, a shrine of Understanding, a portal to the comprehension of the Metaphysical, a conduit by which we seek the Knowledge of the Immortals, the One Truth, Veesnu. That, and we serve waffles.

"Waffles?" I raised an eyebrow.

Indeed. We find that waffles contain sufficient carbohydrate and fat levels to make them appealing to species of numerous biological makeups. They are a perfect fuel to allow the Knowledge-hungry Pilgrim to absorb the teachings of Veesnu. Also, rents in the spaceport are high, and we must pay to keep the lights on.

"Gotcha," I said. "Well, I'm not sure we're particularly interested in any enlightenment at the moment, but some waffles would certainly hit the spot right about now." My stomach growled in agreement.

I do not understand your choice of pronoun, human. Your companion does not appear to require sustenance, and if my assumptions are correct, he is not susceptible to enlightenment, as he has already cheated the cosmos. The Dirax clacked its pincers twice.

I started to formulate a question in my mind, but Paige stopped me halfway. *Don't ask. It's complicated. Suffice it to say the Veesnu religion has some pretty strong thoughts about artificial intelligence.*

"Right, waffles for one, then," I said. "I take them with extra butter and syrup. My partner here will have to sustain himself off the negative energies of preju-dice."

I don't think the Dirax got the joke. *We only have room at the bar. Given your anatomy, I assume this is accept-able?*

"Of course." Normally, I would've preferred a booth, but given our need to question the Dirax about Valerie's case, a spot at the bar would serve us swimmingly. We followed the big insect and plopped ourselves onto a pair of the puffy, lipstick-colored stools.

The Dirax disappeared behind an alcove, and within a minute, it returned with a steaming plate of golden-brown cross-hatched carb bombs drenched in cow fats and a slurry of lab-perfected complex sugars designed to evoke flavors of maple, honey, fruit, and the warmest memories of my childhood.

I sawed off a piece and plunged it into my mouth, the flavor molecules exploding as they contacted my tongue.

Carl looked at me longingly. "See, there's another experience I sometimes envy you."

"What are you talking about?" I said around a mouth-ful of hot buttered bliss. "You can taste things."

"Yes, but then I'd either have to suffer the indignity of spitting out my food or empty my catch container, which is a pain to service. Either way I'd have to clean my mouth afterwards."

"You sure are surly today," I said.

"Maybe that firmware upgrade I got is malfunction-ing, after all," said Carl.

I tilted my head as I stuffed another slice of waffle in my mouth. "Won't work this time, old pal. Now I know you're joshing me."

The Dirax loomed over us on the other side of the counter. *Is there anything else I can provide you with? Perhaps a lecture on the interwoven nature of organic and cosmic systems, and how an acceptance of Veesnu can bring peace to the neural systems that dictate your actions?*

I swallowed and lifted a finger. "Not that, no, but we do have a couple questions for you, if you don't mind."

The Dirax twitched its antennae. *Such as?*

"We're looking for someone."

Who?

"I don't know."

Can you provide a description?

"Not really."

What about a digital imprint of their neural pathways?

"Huh? No, definitely not."

The Dirax clacked its pincers again. *I am confused.*

I sighed. "You're not the only one, brother. We don't know exactly who we're looking for, but they left us a clue leading back to your establishment. A slip." I pulled out the card we'd liberated from the sock at Keelok's and showed it to the Dirax.

Ah. Yes. We give these to all individuals who enter our doors. I was going to provide you with one at the conclusion of your meal.

"Could you take a closer look at this one in particular?" I asked. "Maybe there's something special about it."

I do not understand your query. What could be more special than the One Knowledge, the metaphysical Truth, the combined teachings of Veesnu, concentrated onto a small, portable slip?

I frowned as I glanced at Carl. "Why is it aliens have issues understanding the meaning of that word? No, that's not what I meant, Mr....?"

Names are not a convention of our species.

"Um...right then," I said. "What I was wondering was if you noticed any features that distinguished this particular slip from others you've distributed."

The Dirax's antennae twitched. I do not know who I provided this slip to, if that is the crux of your query.

I rapped the knuckles of my right hand onto the palm of my left. "Argh. How are we supposed to track someone down when we have no name, physical description, or identifying qualities whatsoever?"

"Patience, Rich," said Carl. "This is the sort of work your profession entails. It's par for the course, I believe."

"I don't know," I said. "All the old P.I. novels I read that got me interested in this gig had a lot more action and a lot less head scratching—though roughly the same number of attractive women. I guess I should be glad we haven't encountered any cats yet, right?"

Carl nodded before turning to the Dirax, who apparently didn't possess the same facial agility we did otherwise it would've looked extremely confused. "One more question for you, if you don't mind. Did a patron of yours happen to lose a sock here in the past couple days, by chance?"

Socks are the tubular coverings your species places over its extremities for warmth?

"Correct," said Carl.

I am unsure. Perhaps. We do have a small lost and found in back. You should check with my broodmate. The Dirax pointed to a slim door behind the pulpit in the chapel half of the room.

"Good thinking, Carl," I said. "And thanks for the help, bud."

It is my pleasure to assist all Pilgrims, human. But I would be remiss not to express again the wonders of the One Truth, the ultimate Knowledge, Veesnu. The wonders of the cosmos await. Verily—

I crammed the last of the waffles in my mouth and stood, pointing at my full mouth and making hand gestures I hoped would translate somewhere along the lines of 'can't talk, busy eating,' neglecting the obvious fact that I could communicate with the Dirax solely via Brain instead of speaking. It might've been a crude exit, but it got me to the back door without having to endure any more of the restaurateur's pushy sermons.

7

We found the second Dirax at a standing desk in the back, surrounded by sacks of flour, stacks of empty egg cartons, and boxes upon boxes full of Veesnu proselytization slips. I almost did a double take when I saw the guy. I thought my buddy the waffle artist from in front had scurried around and beat us to the punch, but Paige quickly quashed my theory that the guy was a closet schizophrenic.

Just because you can't tell the differences between them doesn't mean they're the same individual, she said. *This one's scutellum is markedly more pronounced than that of the Dirax you previously met, as is its petiole, and the funiculi on its antennae are more bumpy and textured to boot.*

I kindly informed Paige that I had no clue what the hell she was talking about.

Bah, she said. *You couldn't tell the difference between a piebald mare and a tan gelding.*

Not wanting to admit that I didn't know what those were either, I cleared my throat as we approached the

Dirax and its hard, glossy shell. The large, insectoid creature declined to turn to greet us.

You appear to be lost, the Dirax voice sounded in my mind. *The restroom is located in the front.*

"What? No, I'm not here for that." I glanced at Carl. "Why does everyone assume I'm looking for a bathroom?"

The Dirax turned. *Pardon, human, but from my knowledge of the physiology of your kind, I was led to believe a harsh expelling of gas such as you exhibited was a sign of gastrointestinal distress.*

"Huh?" I said. "Oh, no, I was clearing my throat. It's an expression we use to attract attention. The action you're thinking of comes from a...different orifice."

Ah. My apologies. The Dirax crossed its pincer arms. *Nonetheless, the spiritual and gustatory experiences we offer take place in the front of our establishment.*

"I know," I said. "But we're here looking for something. Your boy toy in front told us you had a lost and found."

Boy toy?

"Friend? Acquaintance? Confidant? Broodmate? The guy selling waffles."

I see. You were using a human term of endearment. I will have to remember this one for future reference. But my thinking has veered tangentially. Yes, we have a lost and found. What have you displaced?

"A sock," I said. "Do you have it?"

It would depend. Can you describe it?

"I don't know. It's a sock. We think a friend of ours lost it here."

The Dirax clicked its pincers, a tic I was starting to think could express any number of emotions from disapproval to annoyance. *You are here to retrieve an article of clothing that does not belong to you? I am unfamiliar with many human customs, but this seems unethical to me.*

"No, it's not like that. This woman, Valerie Meeks, she hired us to investigate—"

The Dirax stuck a pincer in the air. *No. I cannot allow it. Apologies and best wishes to you.*

I gritted my teeth. Dealing with aliens could be a test of composure and patience—two personality traits I wasn't particularly adept at. Back in my kickboxing days, I'd succeeded in most of my bouts mainly by adopting a devil-may-care attitude, intimidating my competition, and attacking like crazy. I'd mellowed in my early-middle age, but I still didn't do well with curtness. Thankfully, Carl rescued me from my own temper before it boiled over.

"We *can* describe the article in question if it makes a difference," he said. "We're looking for a sock of roughly this length—" He measured it out with his hands. "—and white in color, with a blue stripe across the toes."

"How do you know any of that?" I asked.

"That's the match to the other mismatched sock from Miss Meeks' dresser," said Carl. "It only makes sense the other sock was misplaced here."

I tried to figure out how I hadn't made that connection while the Dirax contained to act as if whatever organ inside of its body that performed the actions of a heart was made of stone. *No. I cannot let you have it. It is not appropriate.*

"We don't actually need the sock," continued Carl. "We just need to look at it."

The Dirax waggled its antennae as it considered our request. *Very well. I do not see how a visual inspection of the article would violate any social conventions of ownership. I will show you what we have.*

The large insect creature turned and shuffled toward a wall-mounted shelf from which it pulled a small box about the same size as two loaves of bread pressed side to side.

"This is your lost and found?" I asked.

Yes. The Dirax opened the box and held it forward.

I snorted as I took stock of the contents. "You've got to be kidding me."

The creature leaned forward. *Do you now require the restroom?*

"No. That snort was another expressive mechanism," I said. "And please stop asking me about that. It's weird. But I'm starting to wonder if this is all some big joke between you, your friend, and me."

I don't understand.

I reached into the box and pulled out a length of white cotton. "This sock is the only bloody thing in the box! Of course this is what we're looking for!"

Please be gentle, intoned the Dirax. *We agreed to a visual inspection only.*

I sighed and let Carl and his delicate hands take over. He poked at the bottom of the sock, then reached in and pulled out another slip, similar to the one for the Veesnu chapel we'd found at the Funporium except this one exhibited a much more businesslike aura, with a name, an address, and an insignia printed upon it in a bold typeface.

You cannot retain that, the Dirax's voice instructed. *By being within the sock, it is considered property of the rightful owner. At least I believe that is how proprietorship would be applied in this case. Sort of a chicken and egg scenario, no?*

"I think you're mixing metaphors," I said. "But it's all right. We're not going to take the slip. We only want to look at it."

Carl handed it over so I could get a closer look. The slip listed a Dr. Francis Castaneva, Professor of Exoneurobiology at Cetie University in Pylon Alpha. An address was listed underneath the name.

"Anything I'm not seeing here, Paige?" I asked.

There's a bunch of promotional research vids on the slip, she said. *Fun stuff. You can watch them on the climber trip back to Cetie.*

Fun. Right, I thought.

I handed the card back to the Dirax, who accepted it with a surprisingly gentle claw. After giving the creature a somewhat insincere thanks and suffering through another misinformed lecture on human property law, I ushered Carl back into the spaceport hallway, managing to escape before the waffle vendor tried to sell us on any more Veesnu mumbo-jumbo.

I stuck my hands in my pockets as we walked back toward the climber, a frown working its way onto my face despite my best efforts to the contrary.

Carl noticed. "You're rather surly for a guy who had the next clue to his case delivered to him on a silver platter."

"Yes," I said. "And that's precisely why I'm surly."

Carl raised an eyebrow.

I tried to elaborate. "Doesn't this seem odd to you?"

"Many aspects of this case seem odd," he said. "To what in particular were you referring?"

"Everything," I said. "I mean, we already established how strange it is that someone broke into Valerie's apartment and instead of stealing anything, other than a pair of socks apparently, they organized the joint and left behind a mystery token. That behavior's odd enough, but everything we've found since? It's as if the perpetrator intentionally left a trail of breadcrumbs for us to follow. What kind of thief—or not-a-thief, if you will—wants to get caught? And if they want to get caught, there are easier ways to go about it. They could've sent Valerie a ping or showed up at her doorstep and confessed."

Carl nodded. "It would appear we're being intentionally strung along. The question is why, and to what end?"

"Exactly." I snapped my fingers a few times, but no revelations spontaneously popped into my head. "Oh well. We should probably tell Valerie what we have and haven't found. Paige, can you connect us?"

A trill sounded in the back of my mind, the distinctive sound of a Brain call. It rang five, six, seven times. "Um, Paige?"

The trill stopped.

Sorry, Paige said. *Looks like Miss Meeks declined the call.*

I looked at Carl. "Hmm."

"She must be busy," he said. "Try again later."

My android friend was probably right, but the conspiracy theorist in me wondered if perhaps Valerie hadn't answered for a different reason. What if the intruder had intentionally led us on a wild goose chase to isolate Valerie and place her in a vulnerable position? Could my precious flower of a client be in danger?

That's a ridiculous notion and you know it, said Paige. *If someone were after Valerie, why would they wait until you were involved before going after her?*

Paige had a good point, but I still couldn't get the thought off my mind. At least, not until Paige bored me to sleep with neurobiological research vids she'd culled from the cardslip during the climber ride back to Pylon Alpha.

8

"Ah, college," I said. "The camaraderie, the pageantry, the passion! These hallowed grounds sure take me back."

We walked down the campus's west mall, a broad expanse of walkways and manicured grass hedged by neat rows of knee-high white orchids and canary-yellow birds of paradise. Hanging over them swayed bright red-orange poincinias, more commonly known as flame trees, their boughs heavy with so many blossoms I could barely discern the green leaves underneath the brilliant crowns of vermilion.

I took a deep breath, filling my nostrils with the sweet, sticky scent of the flowers and the damp, earthy aroma of the freshly cut grass, though other smells lingered as well. Stale beer and old urine, I think.

"Um, Rich, I hate to break this to you," said Carl, "but you never went to college, much less Cetie U."

"Oh, I know that," I said. "But that doesn't mean I didn't crash my fair share of college parties. And let me tell you, there's a certain liveliness and vivaciousness that erupts at a party full of college co-eds that you don't find anywhere else. It could be the exuberance of youth, or the eagerness of open minds—"

"Or the copious amounts of alcohol consumed," said Carl.

"—or that," I admitted. "But still, good times."

We crossed onto a path lined by rose-colored hibiscus flowers that wound to and fro like a drunken river before spilling out in front of a high-domed building crusted with cornices, balustrades, parapets, and other completely unnecessary details architects seemed intent on cramming onto the front of every academic building they could get their hands on. Perhaps the embellishments' purpose was to lend an air of knowledge and sophistication to buildings that essentially functioned as gathering spots for kids with too much money and time on their hands, but the cynic in me thought the adornments had a more basic purpose—one that resulted in more SEUs in the bank for the architects and builders.

Carl and I shuffled into the building and took a lift to the third floor, working our way down a cream and white hallway edged with elaborate baseboards and crown molding before ending at the address our lost-and-then-found sock-clad slip had indicated.

The door winked open, and we walked into an austere room with only four pieces of furniture in it: three plush chairs and a slim, curved, clear plastic desk that reminded me of a wave cresting upon an invisible shore. Behind the desk, in one of the chairs, a woman sat.

She was short, just over a meter and a half, with big dark eyes and long, chestnut brown hair held in a tight ponytail. The slim nose perched on the front of her face held a bit of a curl to it, but in a natural way, not one forced by awkward manipulative surgery.

On the far wall across from the woman, images from a projector spun and swirled—proteins folding and molecular diagrams assembling. Within the maelstrom sat static equations featuring lots of symbols that weren't a part of the traditional English alphabet.

The woman jabbered away at someone on her Brain as we entered. "—but that's exactly what I told the oversight board. I know they expect a grant proposal in by tomorrow morning, but the problem is we can't submit it without knowing the T-base sequencing mechanics, and our programs to model them haven't finished processing the projections. Unless the dean kicks McDougal off the cluster in the next half hour, I can't imagine we'll be able to finish in time, much less analyze the results."

She finally noticed us. "Hey, can you hold a sec?" She turned toward Carl and I. "My office hours are from oh-fourteen hundred to oh-sixteen hundred on the same days as my lectures."

I glanced at Carl. "Why does everyone always assume they know what I want? First Keelok, then that Dirax, now one of the finest minds Cetie U has to offer. You'd think people would ask more and assume less. You know what they say about people who assume, right?"

"Excuse me?" said the woman.

"Nothing," I said. "We're not students. Are you Professor Castaneva?"

"Well, clearly he's not a student," she said, gesturing at Carl and his robotic physique. "And yes, I am." Her eyes narrowed. "Are you from the funding committee? Maybe *you* can talk some sense into the oversight board. I've been interfacing via Brain with Darna all morning, but she can't seem to get them to grant us an extension. Maybe if—"

"Slow down. I'm not with any board. The name's Rich Weed. I'm a P.I."

"Yeah, so?" she said. "I am, too. Just about everyone on our faculty is. Are you here about a collaboration? Because now's not a good time."

I blinked. "Wait...*what*? You're a private investigator, too?"

"*What*? No." The professor shook her head. "I'm a *principal* investigator. The head of a research project. You're really a private dick?"

"Whoa, watch the language," I said. "Carl here gets easily offended."

"He's joking," said Carl. "He does that a lot. But to answer your question, yes, we are."

"Darna, let me call you back," said Professor Castaneva, waving us in and pointing us toward the two open chairs. "Sorry about that. I've been up to my elbows in grant bullshit all day. Makes me snappy. So you guys are private investigators, huh? I didn't know those still existed."

"Few people do," I said as I took a seat. "We're something of a dying breed, Professor."

"Call me Fran," she said. "Professor Castaneva makes me sound too much like my father. So what's going on? What brings a pair of private eyes my way?"

"We're investigating a case," I said.

Fran raised her eyebrows. "Yeah...I figured as much. I may not have any experience with detective work, but I do have a Ph. D., you know. I was looking for more specifics."

"And, believe it or not, I was trying to avoid them," I said.

"Huh? Why? Are you involved in something lurid?" The professor leaned forward. "Don't tell me there's a sex scandal going on in the department. Not that I'd be that surprised. I've seen the way Professor Doyle looks at some of his grad students."

I shook my head. "Nothing like that. I was avoiding specifics because I have so few of them."

Fran leaned back. "Explain."

"Well, our case is a little...*unorthodox*," I said.

"Which is putting it mildly," said Carl. "Our client hired us to investigate a trespassing that occurred at her apartment, but nothing was taken. Instead, the intruder left behind a clue, ostensibly to help us find him or her."

"It was a token for an antique gaming cabinet," I said. "One that led us to an arcade in the spaceport owned by a Tak named Keelok. Once there, we found another clue leading to a Veesnu church operated by a couple of pair-bonded Diraxi, except the church also served waffles, if you can believe it. And the waffles were good. *Darn* good. But that's not what we were after. We were looking for a sock, and we found it in their lost and found. That led us here."

"A *sock* led you here?" Fran asked, her brows furrowed.

"Well, not precisely. One of your promo slips was inside." I pointed to a desktop slip holder, full of slim, plastic rectangles with the Cetie U logo emblazoned upon them, which faced me from the corner of the professor's workspace. Other than a holoprojector base which looked as if it could be used for displaying anything from vacation stills to brain cross-sections, it was the only thing on her desk.

"One of my slips was in a sock?" Fran glanced at the holder. "You're not just making this up are you?"

"I told you it was complicated," I said.

Fran rubbed her thumb and forefinger across the edges of her thin, pink lips. "You know, I'd be happy to help you, detectives, but I'm struggling to see how I fit in here."

"You're not the only one," I said. "Trust me, I know how this sounds, but unfortunately I've told you pretty much everything we have to go on. You're telling me there's nothing about my story that sounds familiar to you?"

"Gaming tokens? Waffles? Socks containing clues? No, none of that is at all familiar," said Fran. "However, I suppose it *is* rather interesting you found my slip at a Veesnu church. I'm a professor of exoneurobiology, and my area of expertise is in Diraxi brain function."

"So?" I asked. "Veesnu is a Diraxi religion, but what does that have to do with your research?"

"More than you'd think," said Fran. "Through we call Veesnu a religion, it's more of a cross between a theology and a science. There's a lot of principles in it that have their basis in the fundamentals of Diraxi brain function."

"I sense an explanation is heading my way," I said. "I should warn you, I never went to college, so I'm not particularly adept at sciencey stuff."

"It's worse than that," said Carl. "He also spent a number of years taking kicks to the head for a living."

I glanced at my fair-haired partner. "Maybe that firmware update of yours really *is* messing with your circuits. That felt particularly snarky."

"It's a statement of fact," said Carl. "The intent was to inform Professor Castaneva of your learning handi-cap."

I raised an eyebrow.

"You've been medically diagnosed," Carl reminded me.

"I wasn't going to lecture you," said Fran, holding up her hands in appeal. "Honestly, I'm not an expert on Veesnu, though I do find it interesting."

"How so?" I asked, leaning forward.

If you were that curious about the religion, I could've briefed you on your way here, said Paige.

Yes, but you're not cute and fleshy, I thought as I gazed at the Professor's pretty little nose.

"Well, think about it," said Fran. "The Diraxi neural system developed to transmit and receive communica-tions through electromagnetic pulses, which is how they're able to communicate with those of us with Brain implants, but unlike our electronic devices which are tailored to transmit and receive along certain wavelengths, the Diraxi are able to pick up a wide spectrum of transmissions. Think of their antennae as providing them with a sort of sixth sense. Just as we can focus on a smell or sound, they can focus on a particular electronic transmission, but that doesn't mean they don't sense, at some level, the noise around them. And the universe is *full* of electromagnetic radiation, not just from the activities of sentient beings, but from the cosmos itself. You could see how an early Diraxi culture might be inspired to base a religion upon the 'voice of the universe,' as they sometimes call it."

I nodded as I pretended to show interest.

"And as intriguing as all that is," Fran continued, "the really interesting part is how their neural architecture processes and filters the signals. Have you ever noticed how Diraxi communications don't feel the same as incoming Brain missives? Sort of how it feels like they're *thinking* at you instead of *talking* to you in your head? Well, it's because we don't actually require Brains to interpret their communications, only to receive them.

"Normally, when we communicate with other species through auditory cues, our Brains automatically translate the speech into something recognizable, but Diraxi don't bother. Their communications work with our minds at a subliminal level, one that goes beyond speech to mere thought. It's fascinating, really, and even more so because their neural architecture is so different than ours. Honestly, it's far more similar to that present in androids and AIs than human brains, but somehow the Diraxi have been able to adapt their communications to fit human patterns of thought. But I'm rambling. Sorry. I get excited about neurobiology, if you couldn't tell."

I blinked the fog from my eyes and tried to process everything the cute, chestnut-haired professor had told me, but I was having a hard time of it. My plan to show interest in her work as a precursor to wooing her had pretty much failed when she uttered the word 'neural' for a third time.

Paige snickered at me, but I ignored her. "Your passion shines through, Fran, but I'm not sure any of that helps us unravel the case we're working on. I don't suppose there's anything else you could offer us?"

The professor shrugged. "You're going to have to give me some direction. I'm still not entirely sure how I'm involved in any of this."

"Have you ever heard the name Valerie Meeks?" I asked.

She shook her head.

"And nothing from our story earlier rang any bells?"

"Nope."

I scratched my chin. "I don't suppose anyone misplaced any socks around here?"

"Definitely not."

I curled my fingers into a fist and pounded them lightly into my open hand, feeling as if my frustration was dangerously close to boiling over again.

"This is ridiculous," I said to Carl. "How the heck are we supposed to solve a case when we have no suspects, no crime to speak of, and our only clues appear to have been planted by someone with a sock fetish whose primary goal was to make us gallivant all over Pylon

Alpha like a pack of spaced-out knuckleheads? Seriously, I'm starting to second-guess accepting this stupid case in the first place."

I turned to Fran. "I'm sorry for wasting your time, Professor. You were as helpful as you could've been given the circumstances."

"Oh, it wasn't a waste of time at all, Detective," she said. "Honestly, you're the most interesting thing that's walked through my door in weeks. A real live private investigator—very cool. Feel free to contact me via Brain if you need anything going forward."

"Really? Anything?" I asked as I stood. "That's a pretty blank card. What if I need help with a homework assignment?"

Fran lifted an eyebrow and a smile tickled the corner of her lips. *"Anything,* Investigator. Though that wasn't quite what I had in mind."

It took me a moment, but the gears in my head finally caught. *"Oh.* Um, excellent. I'll keep that in mind, and, um...maybe we'll talk later?"

"I'd love to," said Fran. "But not for a couple days, ok? I've got this grant stuff to finish, after all."

I left the professor's office in a bit of a haze, wondering how I'd managed to make such a solid impression on the woman after bumbling my way through our conversation. I was sure I'd proven myself to be completely ignorant of her field of study as well as incompetent at my own job.

Despite his reminder about my long lady drought during our climber ride, Carl apparently decided I needed to get my head out of clouds and back to our maddening case. "So, what now?"

"Now?" I said. "Now we call Valerie and see what the heck is going on, because there's definitely something fishy about this operation we've gotten ourselves sucked into. Paige?"

The trilling in my head started again.

"You think she's involved in this somehow?" said Carl.

"I don't know, but someone knows something we don't, and I'm running out of ideas. Paige, anything?"

Nope, she said. *In fact—yup, she just blocked you.*

The ringing stopped.

"Wait..." I said. "Valerie blocked me from calling her? Are you sure you pinged the right Brain?"

Of course I'm sure, said Paige. *She must still be busy, although I don't know why she wouldn't simply decline the call again.*

Carl and I glanced at each other.

Maybe you were right earlier, said Paige.

"About what?"

Maybe someone did want to get us out of the way for a while, said Paige. *Maybe it was Valerie herself.*

"That doesn't make any sense," I said. "As you said, if she didn't want us involved in her personal business she never would've come calling in the first place. No, there must be something else going on."

I shook my head. Despite my best efforts and the lingering euphoria related to Fran's interest, I couldn't stop the knight in shining armor inside of me from thinking the beautiful, busty Valerie Meeks might be in trouble.

"Let's head back to Val's place," I suggested. "If we can't call her, maybe we can track her down the old-fashioned way."

Nobody else had any better suggestions, so we exited the building and caught a cab to the tube station.

9

Our car dropped us off in front of Valerie's glossy, steel high-rise, and we took the lift back to the fifth floor. During the ride from downtown, I'd had Paige give Valerie's Brain another try, but our call had immediately been declined. Despite having just met the strawberry blonde earlier in the day, and despite the fact that I felt she was somehow yanking my chain, I couldn't help but feel a strange attraction to her—an attraction which, at the moment, manifested itself as concern.

I approached her door and had Paige ring the chimes. As I waited for a response, I stared into the frosted glass and suffered a vision of the future: Valerie and I arguing furiously, me over her lackadaisical approach to her own safety, her over my lack of progress on her case, both of us yelling and pointing fingers and feeling our blood rush and boil before ultimately falling into each others arms' and kissing passionately.

Carl crashed my daydream party. "Hey, Rich?"

I blinked the fog away from my eyes. "Huh?"

"We need to reevaluate our plan."

"Oh, right, right," I said. "You want to try the old good cop, bad cop routine? Or I could pose as the gallant savior and you could pose as the third wheel that gets lost."

Carl gave me a furrowed eyebrow sort of look. "Um...that's not what I meant. The door's ajar."

I followed Carl's finger to where the frame met the door. A slight gap peered through to the other side. While in the throes of my passionate reverie, I'd totally missed it.

Paige wasn't happy about the slight. *Sometimes I wish I had my own sensory inputs.*

I tapped on the Pseudaglas, and a faint clinking rattle sounded from the base.

"Sounds like the actuators are broken," said Carl. "I'd wager someone forced the door."

I tried to jam my fingers into the crack at the side, but they wouldn't fit. Carl, with his slimmer hands, managed to dig his fingernails into the crevice and slide the door to the side. It gave with an unpleasant grating rasp.

"Um, Valerie? Are you here?" I asked as I stepped into the apartment.

I was willing to guess she wasn't. The place had been tossed. Cushions from Valerie's sofas lay discarded haphazardly on her thick, fuzzy rug, exposing the internal ribbing of the chairs. Vases and decorations on her shelves had been pushed to the sides, twisted and turned and upended. The kitchen, however, had seen the worst of it. Pots, pans, and utensils partied on the floor and spilled into the living room like sweaty, drunken revelers on the eve of the Perihelian Festival. A poor dishbot who'd probably been set to work in Valerie's absence rotated back and forth, overwhelmed by the mess, trying to decipher what needed to be stored and where.

"Well, this isn't good," I said.

Really? said Paige. *That's your first thought? No wonder you've struggled in this business.*

Carl must've received the jab, too. "To be fair, we've solved every case that's come our way. Volume's been the problem."

I steamed a little at Paige's insult, but years of practice dodging her jabs helped me brush it off. "Alright. Here's an insight for you. Looks like we were right about there being more people involved in this mess than we originally thought. No way the first intruder, the one who went out of his or her way to leave this apartment spotless after breaking and entering, is responsible for this disorderly mess."

"You're most likely correct," said Carl. "Why don't I inspect the kitchen while you return to the bedroom? Perhaps the newest intruders left clues the previous ones didn't."

I nodded and headed toward Valerie's private quarters. I whistled upon spotting her monument to clothing—her expandable closet. Whoever had trespassed this time clearly didn't hold fashion in the same regard that Val did. The racks had been stripped bare, and her clothes churned over the floor like the waters of a turbulent, parti-colored sea.

Miss Meeks is not going to be happy, said Paige.

"No kidding," I said. "You want to give her another call?"

I'll try, she said, and then a moment later, *No dice. Still blocked.*

I suffered another pang of worry.

But the call is going through, Paige said. *She's just refusing to answer it. I'm sure she's fine.*

I stomped over to the dresser drawer, which I found in a similar state of disarray as the floor. Every pair of socks had been pulled apart and tossed back into the drawer with blatant disregard for Valerie's preferred color- and fabric-based organizational metrics. I sifted through the loose stockings, not entirely sure what I was looking for but certain I hadn't found it.

I heard the patter of Carl's feet and then his voice drifting over from the entrance to the bedroom. "Find anything unusual?"

"No more arcade tokens, if that's what you mean," I said as Carl joined me at my side. "And I doubt we'll find any more of those. This seems like your traditional toss and snatch job. Whoever was here was looking for something. No clue on whether or not they found it, though." I snapped my fingers as I suffered a thought. "Wait...do you think whoever was here was after the token?"

"It's a distinct possibility," said Carl.

I twisted my lips and grunted.

"What?" asked Carl.

"Well, I already put that dang thing in the vintage arcade cabinet," I said. "If this turns into some sort of token ransom situation, I may have screwed the pooch."

"I doubt anyone was after that particular token," said Carl. "As you already mentioned, there wasn't anything special about it. I ran every diagnostic I could, given the circumstances. If the intruders who caused this mess—" Carl waved about. "—were after the token, chances are they were after the same string of clues we already found."

"Ok, but why?" I asked as I scratched my head. "All we found on our goose chase was a pair of socks, a potentially sexually available professor, and another boatload of questions."

"Despite my superior computational power, I'd have to say your guess is as good as mine at this point," said Carl.

"I know as much about something as you do?" I said. "I'll have to file that away for future gloating purposes."

I took another look around at the chaos.

Carl caught the look in my eyes. "Formulating a plan?"

"Not really," I said. "But I do want to talk to Valerie now more than ever. There has to be more to this case than she's letting on."

"Well, then we should probably head to the bakery," said Carl.

Something tickled the back of my brain. "She did say that's where she was going to be, didn't she?"

Carl nodded.

"Damn it, Carl, why didn't you say something before we trekked back here?" I asked. "Not that it turned out to be a bad idea, but still."

Carl shrugged. "I assumed you had an ulterior motive. Like a desire to rifle through Miss Meeks' unmentionables without her knowing."

I sputtered. "*What?* No. It was just socks. Really. But don't tell her."

Carl smiled, and Paige snickered.

"Wait...that was a joke?" I said. "*You.* This firmware upgrade of yours is definitely going to take some getting used to."

I turned tail and headed toward the door.

10

I stared out the cab window watching civilization zip past me in all its shiny and transparent glory—a portrait of humanity painted in metallic silver and clearcoat and wiped into a blur, not by the speed of the car but by the degree of defocus of my own eyeballs.

"Are you ok?"

I peeled my face off the window and turned to Carl. "Huh?"

He sat on the bench seat across from me, his hands clasped lightly in his lap. "I said, are you ok?"

I knit my brows together, trying to get the gist of Carl's comment, but my brain seemed to be functioning at a fraction of the rate of the images blurring across the cab window. "What? Of course. Why wouldn't I be?"

"You remind me of a forlorn puppy trapped inside during a rainstorm," said Carl as he intertwined his fingers.

I snorted and turned back to the window.

"You want to talk about it?" asked Carl.

I shrugged and ignored him for a moment, but eventually I responded. "I can't help but shake a feeling Valerie's in trouble."

"Ah. So your vacant stare is a result of emotional pangs."

I turned back to Carl. "Are you making light of the situation? Because Valerie could be in a serious bind."

"I wasn't," said Carl. "Although I do tend to agree with Paige on this one. It would appear Valerie's voluntarily severed communications for the time being. That alone doesn't indicate anything unseemly occurred."

"And what about her apartment? The break-in?" I asked. "That didn't change your mind?"

"It didn't indicate a kidnapping occurred, if that's your concern," said Carl.

I shook my head. "I don't know. Maybe you're right. Maybe I'm overreacting..."

Carl tilted his head. "But?"

"But what?" I asked.

"I assumed you were leaving something unsaid."

"Maybe I was."

Carl lifted an eyebrow.

I sighed. "Fine. Maybe you were right. Maybe...I'm not cut out for this gig."

Carl untangled his fingers and placed them at his sides. "Why would you say that?"

"A number of reasons," I said. "I keep getting frustrated with the lack of evidence, for one thing. I feel like I haven't made any tangible discoveries or added any crucial insights, either. And there's my budding relationship with Valerie."

"*Budding relationship?*" said Carl.

"Ok, maybe that's a stretch," I said. "Perhaps infatuation would be a better word. But regardless, it's not a good thing. Rule number one: never get emotionally attached to the client. I read that somewhere. Probably one of those old P.I. novels. Seems true enough, though it should probably be rule number two. Rule one should be make sure you get paid upfront. Not sure I've done particularly well on either count."

"While I can't argue with you about that last part," said Carl, "I wouldn't make the connection that your current emotional state makes you unfit for investigation. You've never suffered the same problem before, even if the root cause of your problem has always existed."

"Huh? You mean in the cat cases? What root problem?"

"You've never fallen for a client before," said Carl. "Look, you're a kind hearted individual. You care for others, which can be an advantage or a disadvantage depending on the situation. In most cases it's a boon. It draws you to others, but it also draws them to you."

I looked at Carl askance.

He looked back. "What?"

"I'm processing that," I said. "With all your snarkiness today, I'm trying to figure out if that was sarcasm or not."

"I'm being nothing but honest," said Carl. "Your personality infects most everyone it touches. Take Professor Castaneva."

"Fran?" I said. "It wasn't my personality that infected her. She's only interested in me because I'm a private eye and she thinks my profession is full of covert ops and daring escapes—mystery and intrigue and wonder. Little does she know I spend most of my time sitting around playing Smashblocks while Paige nags me." On command, my ever-present digital lady friend poked me in my temporal lobe. "But my connection with Valerie was different. She actually seemed interested in...*me*."

"What exactly are you basing any of this on?" Carl asked.

"When we were at her place. Alone, in her bedroom, investigating the trespassing," I said. "She gave me a look."

Carl pressed his lips together and furrowed his brows.

"Whatever," I said. "I know what I saw. There was something there."

"If you say so," said Carl.

The cab turned a corner and began to slow.

"Looks like we're almost here," I said.

"Indeed," said Carl. "So are you going to discuss these emotions with Miss Meeks?"

If I'd been sipping a beverage, I would've performed a spit take. Instead, I merely coughed and sprayed a bit of spittle over the synthetic interior of the cab. "*What*? No way. I'm a man. We keep our feelings repressed way down inside where it's dark and cold and they can never get out. Besides, do I need to remind you of rule number one? Or two, or whatever it was? No relationships with the client. This needs to be purely business—and I intend to find out what kind of business we've gotten ourselves into, exactly."

Paige snickered at me. Perhaps she doubted my commitment to professionalism with regards to Valerie.

Admittedly, I might've expressed my feelings to Carl with exaggerated verve, but I did intend to stick to the facts when I talked to Val—even if my eyes might sometimes stray south of her neck.

The cab stopped, and Carl and I let ourselves out onto the sidewalk. The warm Tau Ceti rays slapped me on the neck as heat from the pavement reflected off the ground and rocked me with a stiff uppercut.

Before me, sandwiched between a perfumery and a quaint boutique advertising designer clothes for toddlers, Valerie's store baked, both literally and figuratively, in the afternoon Tau Ceti sun. White and pastel yellow drapes hung from inside the windows, framing stacks of baked goods and a vintage chalkboard listing the day's specials. I glanced at the sign above the front door. It read 'The Cooling Rack.' I wondered if the double entendre had been intentional or not.

As I stood there admiring the sign, Valerie stepped out the front door, which swept shut behind her, puffing slightly as it locked. A display in one of the windows reading 'Open' blinked over to 'Closed.' Valerie had changed since our encounter earlier in the day, opting for a pair of white butt-huggers and a tank top that were slightly more work appropriate and better at hiding errant dustings of flour than her previous ensemble, though they did nothing to mar her delicious curves.

Valerie, perhaps not spotting us, started to walk away. I stopped her with a mild shout. "Valerie! Hey! There you are. We've been trying to get hold of you all day. When you didn't answer your Brain, I..." I stuffed my hands into my slacks pockets. "Well, this might sound silly, but I thought something might've happened to you."

Valerie stopped in her tracks, glancing at me and Carl. "Um...do I know you?"

"What do you mean, do you know me?" I said. "I'm Rich. The detective? You hired us to investigate that break-in of yours."

Valerie shook her head. "I'm...sorry. I think you must have me mistaken for someone else."

I blinked, then I turned to Carl and frowned. "Did you set this up? Hire her to act the part of a needy client? Was this all an excuse to get me out of my seat and moving around, and now that she's been paid she wants nothing to do with me?"

"What? No," said Carl.

"Then what?" I asked as I faced Valerie. "Are you feeling ok, Val? Have you been hitting the mescaline martinis? Suffering from walking blackouts?"

"*Excuse me?*" She blinked and shook her head violently. "How would you—? No. I don't know what you're talking about. Please, go away."

Valerie turned and walked down the street. I followed her.

"We followed the trail from that token, you know," I said. "Led us to a Veesnu Chapel staffed by a cute Diraxi couple and then to a Professor of Exoneurobiology, name of Fran Castaneva. Any of that ring a bell?"

Valerie didn't stop walking, but she did glance back at me. "Wait, Diraxi? *Veesnu?*" Her eyes darted back and forth furiously. "I... I don't know what you're talking about. Please leave me alone."

I pressed forth. "We stopped by your apartment on our way back from the spaceport. Someone busted in and tossed the place. We were worried."

Valerie stopped and turned, her face flush with rage. "You broke into my apartment?!"

Her anger forced me back a step. "What? No. The door was ajar. Someone else got there first. We were just looking for—"

"That's it! I'm calling the police!" she said, her eyes acquiring a wild sort of look. "I don't know who you are or what your game is, but I don't want anything to do with you! If you so much as take one step closer to me I'll scream for your droid to help. Now STAY THE HELL AWAY FROM ME!"

Valerie turned and scrammed, fear and dignity taking their turns wrestling over her actions as she vacillated between a hasty jog and a brisk walk.

Carl, who'd stayed rooted to the ground near Valerie's shop, joined me. "That didn't go so well."

"You weren't kidding, right?" I asked him. "This isn't a weird game you drew up to keep me on my toes?"

"Sadly, no," said Carl. "Although now I know what to get you for your birthday."

"Very funny."

I sighed and rubbed a hand through the hair at the back of my neck. In the heat of the moment, I'd been focused on trying to make sense of Valerie's change of heart, but as I watched her run away, clearly rattled, I felt a crack in my insides. The fantasy I'd been working on outside Val's door caught flame and disappeared in a puff of smoke.

"So...what now?" asked Carl.

"I don't know," I said. "But I think I need a drink."

11

Feeling any better? asked Paige.

"Not really," I said. "That's the thing about alcohol, though. It makes you more depressed. Honestly, you'd think in all the millennia humans have been around we'd have figured out a better drug of choice, but I guess scientists still haven't found another chemical cocktail that makes people want to strip down to their birthday suit, party, and kill themselves all at the same time."

I sat in the sitting room of my three-story penthouse apartment, my feet propped up on a padded ottoman, a glass of rye and bitters clutched in my hand. Sunlight streamed in through the windows on my left, spilling onto the blended silk and wool fibers of the rug beneath me. Despite my limited case load, the spoils from my grandpappy's land lease afforded me a few luxuries the majority of out-of-work schmucks couldn't otherwise afford.

Carl sat on a divan across from me. He swirled a tumbler of whiskey in his hand, the ice cubes clinking against the side of the glass. He wouldn't consume the beverage, but drinking alone made me feel more pathetic than I was, so his empathic sensibilities forced him to play along.

"So is that it?" he asked. "Are we really done for the day?"

"Done with what? Drinking?" I glanced at my Old Fashioned. "Not by a long shot."

"I was referring to the case," said Carl. "Look, I know drowning your sorrows after a perceived rejection is a time-honored human tradition, but we have work to do."

I sipped my cocktail and engaged my neurons. "Wait...are you under the impression we're still employed?"

"Well, not as such," said Carl. "But our investigation is far from over."

"You do remember when Valerie told me to get lost, right?"

"That turn of phrase works better on someone whose memory is fallible," said Carl.

"Then you'll also remember how she threatened to call the police," I said. "I may not be the best at reading members of the opposite sex, but I'm *pretty sure* Valerie doesn't want us involved in her business anymore."

Carl stood and started to pace, his footfalls alternating between claps and silence as he moved between the rug and the bare floor. "I know, but aren't you in the slightest bit intrigued? The planted evidence at her home, the trail leading us to the spaceport and back, and now Miss Meeks' own change of heart? I know you've doubted your own deductive abilities, and perhaps I haven't been encouraging enough of this private investigation venture, but you have to admit—this is by far the most interesting case we've ever had."

I raised an eyebrow. "Is this an attempt to get me to stop drinking?"

"It's not *only* that," said Carl. "Come on, Rich. Where's your sense of curiosity?"

I tapped my chin as the liquor soaked into my brain. Carl did have a point. I hadn't entered private investigation because of the earnings prospects, or for the cachet it might provide me with the ladies—which, contrary to my experience with Professor Castaneva, was usually around the order of absolutely nothing. I'd decided to take up my new enterprise because of the mystery, the intrigue, and the promised thrill of the hunt—that, and the knowledge that by doing so I might be able to help people and make a difference in their lives. Carl was right about that fact. I did care about others. More than I wanted to admit, most of the time. And I still cared about Valerie—a point my handful of whiskey could attest to. But could I help her by solving the case she'd tasked me, even though she wanted nothing to do with me anymore?

"You know, if we stick with this, we're probably not going to get paid," I said.

"Our payment was scheduled to be in bear claws," said Carl.

"A vital resource, if there ever was one."

Carl raised both eyebrows.

"Fine. You've won me over," I said. "I'm curious. And a sense of honor compels me to finish this case, glazed pastries or no. But despite your stirring appeal, we don't know where to turn next."

Carl sat back down, his face bright and eager. Perhaps he secretly wished to solve the case, too. I sometimes forgot that in addition to his base layer of subliminal programmatic coding, he had his own wishes and desires and curiosities, as well.

"The key is Miss Meeks," he said. "I can think of three reasons why she might've treated you as she did. The first is she's crazy—which is a possibility, though that option doesn't match with her displayed behavior earlier today. Despite the claims of many human males, only a miniscule fraction of all women are, in fact, psychotic. The second plausible scenario is she doesn't remember contacting you, and the third is that she's lying. Either of the last two possibilities are compelling."

I rubbed my chin some more. "I have to admit, Valerie did seem nervous when we met her outside her bakery—even more so than an average woman would be when accosted in a street by a lout like me. So either Valerie is suffering from delusions, or she no longer wants us to solve the mystery she contacted us about. Even if the former is true, she must've had a reason for searching us out in the first place." I snapped my fingers and held up a triumphant digit. "That's it. That's our next avenue of investigation. We need to discover the real reason Valerie contacted us."

"Precisely," said Carl.

I set my drink down on the end table next to my sofa and rubbed my hands in glee, my despondency disappearing like the chill between my warming fingers. "Well, this should be fun. Just like in the old stories. So, what should we do first? Tap her comm links? Find her and tail her? Put the squeeze on her?"

Oh, I'm sure you'd like to squeeze something of hers, said Paige.

"Tapping into her communications is both beyond our abilities and illegal," said Carl. "Tailing her might be productive but would require too much 'legwork,' as your antiquated detective inspirations might say. I was thinking we'd start with something a little more orthodox. A research report."

"You want to put together a dossier?" I asked. "Well, that's not quite as much fun, but we've got tools at our disposal that shouldn't make it too painful. Paige, you want to help?"

Given Paige's nearly limitless computational power, a slew of information on virtually any person in existence was but a thought away. Of course, Paige could only provide me with data present in the public record, but thanks to the tireless efforts of marketing and solicitation companies as well as freely shared tidbits people posted to social media, that included quite a bit of information.

Alright, let's see here, said Paige. *Miss Meeks' full given name is Valerie Constance Meeks, age two hundred and nineteen—*

I whistled. "She's almost two bills and a score?"

Modern medical technology is a miracle, isn't it? said Paige. *As I was saying, she's two hundred and nineteen. A Cetie lifer. Been off planet a few times, based on her photo streams, but hasn't left in over a decade. Bought her condo about forty-five years ago. Paid a share over market price, but*

given the housing boom Pylon Alpha and its suburbs were suffering at the time, it's been a pretty good investment. Price has
gone up about three-fold since—

"Hey, Paige, this is great stuff," I said, "but seeing as
you're overflowing with algorithms whose primary purposes are filtering information, why don't you put those
circuits of yours to good use and just relate the juicy
bits."

Paige sent me the digital equivalent of a sigh. Oh,
Rich. What would you do without me?

"Probably fail to get the coffee machine started and
lock myself out of my own apartment," I said. "But that's
neither here nor there. Now—the useful stuff, please."

Well, there is something interesting I've gathered from Miss
Meeks' public profiles, she said. Apparently she recently
broke up with her boyfriend, one Gerrold Stein.

"And, other than telling me she's available, this is
interesting how?" I asked.

Because Mr. Stein only shows up in a few standard public
government records. Other than that, he's a virtual ghost. The
only mentions of him are through Miss Meeks' feeds, though I
did manage to scrape a photo of him from Valerie's PhotoHog
app. Here.

Paige flashed me the image via Brain—that of a sun-
tanned, bearded guy with a hook nose and long, black
unwashed dreads.

"Oh, dear lord," I said. "He's one of those anti-
establishment types. Who wants to bet he grows his
own food in a hydroponic vat powered off the fumes
from his hookah and his own idealism?"

Your guess is closer than you think, said Paige. His public
record lists an address way outside the city smack dab in the

middle of an agricultural field, as far I can tell from satellite imagery. Nighttime images of the same area don't show any light pollution, and...yup, Pylon Power and Main doesn't even service that area. This guy's totally off grid.

Something clicked for me upstairs. "What kind of odds do you want to offer me this guy's Brainless?"

Extremely poor ones, said Paige. *Mostly because I already looked him up in the personal listings and found nothing.*

"And if he's Brainless," I said, "that would mean there'd be a number of things he could and couldn't do. He couldn't, for example, play interactive Brain games. He might, instead, be forced to play ancient, token-powered arcade cabinets if he needed a fix. On the other hand, he *could* break into someone's apartment without there being any police Brain record of his presence."

Carl nodded, having followed Paige's half of the conversation through his own feed. "I suppose that's plausible, though I'm struggling to see why an unBrained, anti-technology type would suffer through, in all likelihood, multiple cab rides, a tube ride, and a climber ride all so he could get to a spaceport to play a vintage video game."

"Admittedly, it seems like a stretch," I said. "But someone went to that trouble, Brain or no. And this Stein fellow's breakup with Valerie might be the motive that spurred the break-in. Paige, how long ago did these two lovebirds call it quits?"

About three months ago, if you can believe Valerie's profiles, Paige said.

"Hmm. That's more than I would've expected for a passion-driven retaliatory action," I said. "But who knows. Maybe it took that long for Stein to walk to Val's place from his dirt farm."

"You do realize this is all blatant speculation," said Carl, "and none of this explains why Mr. Stein would plant evidence in Valerie's apartment. Or why someone would later turn her place inside out in an attempt to find said evidence. Or even what said evidence is supposed to point to—which, despite our sojourn to downtown Pylon Alpha and the thermosphere, we still don't have any idea about."

"You're right," I said. "It doesn't. But seeing as my lady-crush Valerie expressed interest in rearranging the position of my testicles if I talked to her again, I figure asking somebody *else* some questions might be a worthwhile avenue to pursue. This Gerrold guy seems like as good a choice as any. So what do you say? You up for a trip to the country?"

12

O ur car rumbled over the dirt road, transforming every pebble and divot into a jerk that sent me bouncing to and fro over my bench seat.

"This is ridiculous," I said to Carl, as we hit a bump that sent me a good two centimeters into the air. "I knew these unBrained hippies were anti-technology, but pavement? Really? I thought they drew the line at electronics."

The jostling didn't bother Carl, but he didn't have various fluid-filled organs inside of him. "I doubt they get around much, to be honest. And it's not merely the unBrained who travel these paths. They're meant for agrarian transport. Tractors and plows tear up roads."

After leaving the tube station, we'd hopped into a cab and directed the car to take us to the spot Paige had found in her surveys—the purported home of Gerrold Stein. We'd found smooth sailing for the first half hour, travelling along blissful traffic-free stretches of elevated roadway, but eventually we'd exited and turned into a maze of corn and wheat fields stretching as far as the eyes could see—which amounted to about the length of my arm. The stalks of grain were nearly three meters tall.

"Still, it seems terribly inconvenient," I said. "You'd think the urban planners would've taken the occasional city slicker corn field expedition into consideration when they planned their agrarian supply chains."

Stop your grousing, said Paige. *We're almost there.*

With all the subtlety of a kick to the face, the stalks outside my window ended, and my fore field of view was restored—at least partially. In the place of the tall, maize-laden stalks, a grove of mangos—a short and squat breed considering the genus—stretched into the seemingly never-ending fields. After passing a few rows of the trees, their boughs heavy and low to the ground with fruit, our car skidded to a halt.

"This is it?" I asked.

This is it, said Paige. *Or at least as close as we can get in a moving vehicle. You'll have to cross the rest of this harsh terrain using those paddle-like implements attached to your ankles.*

"I don't see anything but mango trees," I said.

"No, there's definitely something out there," said Carl. "Hard to see with all the trees in the way, though. Paige, let's move the car forward a bit."

Paige rerouted the request to the car, and it inched forward. The scene outside the window moved at a crawl, the lines of trees shifting like shadows in the late day sun.

"There. Stop." The car did as Carl requested. The droid leaned forward and positioned his head down and to his right. Something flickered in his pupils as his eyes zoomed and focused. "Yes, I see someone. Multiple people, actually. Off in the distance."

"Really? More than one?" I asked.

Well, it makes sense, said Paige. *There's a number of people besides Mr. Stein who all list this patch of land as their address.*

"Great. A whole clan of Brainless hippies. You could've mentioned this earlier. Carl, move. Let me see." I brushed my pal to the side while I shifted to his side of the cab.

"Despite your regular checkups with GenBorn, I doubt your eyes are *that* good," he said.

"Oh, ye of little faith. Despite your constant mockery, I did, in fact, anticipate a scenario such as this before we left."

I reached into the front shirt pocket of my guayabera and produced a slim black case with a microfiber coating. I cracked it open and produced a pair of connected lenses which I settled over my nose.

"Spy glasses," I said. "They'll help me see whatever it is you were peering at. Now move aside and let a master work."

"The term is spyglass," said Carl. "And those are binoculars."

"Whatever." I tapped at the side of my glasses, trying to figure out how to work the suckers. So far, all I'd succeeded in was blurring my vision.

"It would probably help if you put them on properly," said Carl.

"Huh?"

They're backwards, said Paige.

"Dagnabbit," I said, ripping the glasses off and turning them around. "There should be a sign on these things or something."

"Well, one side is convex and the other concave," said Carl.

"Not good enough," I said. "They should be idiot proof."

Implying what exactly? said Paige with a snicker.

I removed the foot from my mouth and held my tongue. Leaning into the spot where Carl had made his discovery, I scrunched my nose and scanned the horizon.

"Yes. There they are," I said. "I think I see them. A group of portly ladies, wearing yellow and orange sarongs, all clustered together."

"Those are the mangos," said Carl.

I gritted my teeth. "You've got to be kidding me. Paige, help me figure this dang contraption out."

I thought you'd never ask.

The glasses finally focused, and a blinking spot appeared in the corner of my eyes. I turned to look at it, and the glasses automatically zoomed. In the distance, I spotted a modest one story log home with a roof fashioned out of dried grass. Outside the structure, a string looped between two poles bore the weight of several soggy articles of clothing, and a pit with charred embers smoldered nearby. There appeared to be several more homes clustered behind the first, but the intruding boughs of the mango trees made it hard to tell.

As I watched, people flitted in and out of my field of view, men and women both. Most wore simple cotton shifts paired with shorts or skirts, and their bodies were muscled and tan, most likely from laboring in the fields. That they did their own labor instead of relegating the tasks to droids was difficult enough to comprehend, but another aspect of them jumped at me with even graver implications.

Some of them were tied together at the wrists—with colorful sashes, oddly enough, but still. And not one, but many. Always a man to a women.

I lifted the glasses off my nose. "Carl, did you see that? The people? Some of them...they're bound together."

"What? I didn't notice that."

"Yes," I said. "At the wrist. Male to female. Why, it's almost as if..." I gasped. "That's what this is all about. Oh my god! They're human traffickers!"

Rich, come on... said Paige.

"That must be the connection with Valerie," I continued. "They tried to take her, but she got away, and now they're after her. The whole relationship angle was a front to keep things quiet when she went missing."

"That's ridiculous," said Carl. "If she was a human trafficking escapee, she would've gone to the police and stayed there. And she would've been truthful about her situation if she'd somehow come to us. Not to mention human traffickers are in the business of kidnapping, not rifling through sock drawers."

I couldn't deny my partner's statements, but my intuition had been piqued and couldn't easily be rerouted. "Good points, all of them. But I know what I saw, and my gut tells me something very, *very* wrong is going on over there. Now, come on. You have a responsibility to serve and protect. Come help me scout this place out so we know what we're up against."

I opened the doors and stepped into the Cetie heat before Carl could dissuade me. I snuck across the grassy expanse between the trees, sliding from trunk to trunk to keep myself from being seen. It proved easy behind the big, leafy mangos, but after a few dozen trees, the orchard switched over to apples, which didn't provide as much trunk cover.

I paused behind a particularly fat specimen, waving Carl over to me.

"See? There they are," I hissed, pointing toward the compound. A couple bound at the wrist in neon green fabric passed through our view.

"The woman doesn't appear to be in any sort of distress," said Carl. "In fact, I'd dare say she looks happy."

"Mind tricks," I said. "Perhaps the victims are suffering from capture-bonding with their jailers. Or they're hopped up on shrooms and goofy pills."

I tiptoed across another grassy expanse and angled my body to the side, reducing my profile as I slipped behind another tree.

Carl followed me without any pretense of stealth. "This is ludicrous. And your attempts at subtlety are unnecessary. If they haven't spotted us, it's entirely due to their own incompetence."

"What are you talking about?" I said. "I'm like a whisper on the wind. Now get behind this trunk before they see us."

Carl sighed and moved behind me while I stuck my head out to get a better look. We'd closed within about a hundred meters of the camp. The captives and their kidnappers had assembled into a large circle, surrounding a young pair in the middle. I wasn't sure what was going on, but I was becoming more and more certain drugs were involved. Many of the participants seemed oddly cheerful.

As I tried to understand the ritual unfolding before me, I heard a buzzing and felt a prick at my neck. I shooed whatever insect was in pursuit of my delectable blood, but the buzzing persisted. Then the blighter had the nerve to bite me. I yelped and slapped my exposed skin.

"Son of a...these damn mosquitoes are going to give us away," I said, wiping my now sticky hand on my slacks. "This is why I rarely leave the city."

"Um...Rich? We may have a problem," said Carl.

"What? Don't tell me the cultists heard me?" I glanced back around the tree toward the camp.

"No," said Carl. "That wasn't a mosquito. That was a bee."

"So? I'm not allergic."

"It appears you're not particularly well-versed in apiculture either."

Another couple of bees buzzed around in the leaves above my head. "Say what?"

"Beekeeping," said Carl. "Are you aware of the genetic modifications between Africanized bees and regular honey bees that occurred in the late twenty-fifth century to help combat dwindling populations?"

"Get to the point, Professor," I said.

"Agricultural pollinization bees are highly territorial, intelligent, and emit potent alarm pheromones.

They also don't lose their stingers or venom sacks upon attack."

The pair of bees in the tree above had morphed into an angry swarm. A number buzzed and flew around my face.

"So, what you're saying is—" Another bee stung me in the cheek. "Yah!"

"Run!" said Carl.

A quick succession of stings to my head and neck overcame any qualms I might've had about revealing myself to the unBrained hippies. I tore out of the boughs of the apple tree like a bat out of hell. My first instinct sent me racing toward the car, but a wave of bees materialized out of thin air and met me before I could reach the mangos. Panicking, I spun and run back the way I'd come, slapping and waving my arms as more bees surged at me from all directions.

Quick, to your left, said Paige, her voice barely audible over the swarming anger of the bees. *There's an irrigation ditch. Dive into it.*

In my distressed state, I didn't question her decision making. I took off in the general direction she'd indicated while irate bees and overzealous apple trees slapped and stung and grabbed at me with equal verve.

There, said Paige.

I dove, expecting a splash.

I got a thump. Thick mud that reeked of decay and tasted like the inside of a boot sprayed into my mouth as my forearms and face made contact with the ditch floor. Bees hummed above me, granting me a temporary reprieve from their stinging as they paused to laugh at my asinine belly flop into the mostly dry creek bed.

Sorry about that, said Paige. *The satellite images must've been out of date. But this could still work. Try smearing that mud over yourself. The bees seem to dislike the odor.*

I wanted to make a remark about how they weren't the only ones, but I followed Paige's advice, rolling around in the rancid, foul-smelling paste and smearing it across my face and forearms. As I did so, a mechanical sound interrupted the buzz of the bees—liquid spraying through a nozzle. I felt a cool mist settle over my neck, and the buzzing subsided.

I looked up. Standing at the lip of the ditch, next to Carl of all people, was a pony-tailed hippie, holding a backpack-mounted sprayer. A clear liquid dripped from the tip of the nozzle.

I offered a salutation. "Um...hi?"

The pony-tailed one raised an eyebrow and frowned.

I gulped.

13

I sat in a primitive sweat lodge, a squat, dark, hovel of a building slapped together out of sticks and dirt and hippie spit. Steam from a rock pit curled around my bare toes. It mixed with smoke from burning embers and licked the soles of my feet before running along my legs and diving under the towel wrapped loosely around my waist. Sweat dripped from my brow, falling in heavy drops onto my bare chest. I took a deep breath, filling my lungs with moist, sticky air.

"Feels good, doesn't it?" I asked.

Carl sat across from me, similarly clad in nothing but a rough, white towel. "I've never understood the appeal of saunas, to be honest. Then again, I don't sweat, so perhaps there's a sensory experience associated with them I'm missing."

"You didn't have to join me," I said. "Your clothes weren't covered in mud."

Carl leaned forward and grasped a small cup. He dipped it into a bucket and poured the contents over the hot stones, letting loose another cloud of steam. "I know."

The motive for his choice to accompany me into the dark, sweat hovel remained unspoken, but I knew the reason. "Carl?"

"Yes?" he said.

"Thanks."

He nodded. He knew what I meant, too.

As it turned out, Carl had been right. The long-haired, unBrained hippies hadn't been involved in human trafficking. Rather, they'd been hosting a wedding—a wedding I'd so unceremoniously crashed. Instead of a cruel restraint, the colorful ribbons I'd noticed tied around everyone's wrists were part of a community hand-fasting ceremony for the young couple undergoing their nuptials.

The ceremony had progressed to about the halfway point when they noticed my yelps and heard me crashing through the orchard like a blind buffalo. Carl, having never suspected the hippies were involved in any for-profit kidnapping schemes, went to the camp for help. There, he managed to find the community beekeeper who doused me with aerosolized bee pheromones—essentially catnip for the little black and yellow pollination machines.

Despite the beekeeper's frown and the fact that I'd trespassed on their property, angered their bees, damaged a number of apple trees, and ruined a wedding, the hippies turned out to be quite the friendly bunch. Instead of stringing me up by my thumbs, they'd gone out of their way to offer me assistance. They hosed me and my mud-caked clothes off, gave me a sticky, home-brewed cream they claimed was a remedy for bee stings, and, while my duds dried on their primitive but effective clothing lines, they ushered me and my naked bottom into one of their sweat lodges.

I took another deep breath of the hot steam and smoke mixture and my brain reeled momentarily. I started to wonder how hot it was inside the lodge and if such an experience might be dangerous, but I didn't have long to ponder. As sweat poured down my chest, a heavy, canvas flap leading to the outside peeled open. A tall, weather-beaten man with dreadlocks and a bushy beard admitted himself, a towel draped around his mid-section. He settled himself across from Carl and I, our spread legs forming an invisible and yet wholly unsettling equilateral triangle.

"Nice little hut, isn't is?" the man said.

I nodded. "Hot, but nice. Yeah."

"The steam's good for those stings, too," he said.

I glanced at one of the bumps on my arms. I thought ice might be a better countermeasure to the stings than heat, but I wasn't about to say so. "Are you Gerrold Stein, by any chance?"

The man nodded. "Heard you wanted to talk to me. Sorry for keeping you waiting."

"Are you kidding?" I leaned forward. "I'm the one who needs to apologize. I feel like a complete fool. When I spotted your ceremony with the ribbons...well, it doesn't matter what I thought. Let's just say my imagination got the best of me. I didn't mean to crash your festivities. Honest. And then the bees came after me, and—"

"Relax, friend," said Gerrold. "It's alright. We're a pretty easy going bunch."

I slumped and settled my back against the wall. "Yeah, I suppose you must be. But really, I'd be happy to pay you back for any damages."

"No need," he said. "Pay it forward to someone else in need. Although, there is one thing I require from you."

"Name it," I said.

"I could use a name, friend."

"Oh. Right. I'm Rich. Rich Weed. This is Carl."

Carl nodded.

Gerrold raised an eyebrow. "Weed, eh? As in related to *the* Weed family?"

"The ones who founded the ganja fields north of Pylon Alpha back in the day? Yeah."

Gerrold tipped his head. "Well, then, I guess I owe *you* thanks, friend. Welcome, both of you."

I didn't have to inquire what he meant by the first part. One look at his dreads spoke volumes about his preferred pastimes, but I was curious about the last part. I shared a look with Carl.

Gerrold noticed the shared glance. "I'm not sure what you may have heard about us, here, but we don't have it out for droids. As a matter of fact, we have no objection to them whatsoever."

"Is that so?" I asked.

Gerrold clasped his hands in his lap before him. His towel sagged under the weight of his grasp, stretching the towel and revealing an uncomfortable amount of leg. "We choose to live simply here, Rich. We don't begrudge those who choose otherwise, so long as they afford us the same luxury of choice."

That seemed a noble philosophy, one that required a thoughtful response, but my brain felt muffled, as if it was slowly being packed with cotton, so I responded with all the wit I could muster. "Hmm. Ok."

Gerrold stretched his arms to the sides, resting them on a lip at chest height. "So..."

"So, indeed," I said.

Gerrold chuckled. "I meant, I assume you're here for a reason. Care to share?"

"Ah, right," I said. "Well, believe it or not, Carl and I are private investigators."

"We have a license and everything," Carl said.

I chuckled. "That we do. And as it turns out, we recently accepted a case from a new client. Valerie Meeks."

Gerrold put a hand up to stroke his beard. "Ah. Well, that's a name I haven't heard in a while."

"We understand she was your girlfriend."

"Sort of," said Stein. "We were close. But I haven't seen her in about three months."

"Do you mind if we ask what happened?" said Carl.

"No. Not at all." Gerrold tugged at some loose beard hairs. "Although, let's see...how should I put this? I suppose she left because she couldn't find what she was looking for."

I must've looked befuddled, because Gerrold took pity on me and explained himself. "As I said, we live a simple life here. As difficult as it may be for you to believe, that appeals to a lot of people, especially those who've spent the majority of their lives in the hustle and bustle of the city. It's not uncommon for strays, even those well into their two hundreds, to search us out. Most only stay for a few days, or perhaps a week. We let them. That's fine. It's part of their journey. Others stay permanently, becoming brothers and sisters. Then...there are those like Valerie.

"When Valerie came to us, she seemed lost, as so many others do. But she had a good heart. I liked her. I'm not sure if we could be considered a couple, but we cared for each other. I taught her about our ways, our lifestyle. She expressed a great interest in our system of Tao Chi."

"I think you mean Tai Chi," said Carl.

"No, Tao Chi," said Gerrold. "It's a comprehensive belief system combining the focus on physical fitness and emotional wellbeing of Tai Chi with the teachings of Taoism. Valerie was particularly interested in the latter. She and I had many powerful discussions over the nature of qi—how it affects our corporeal bodies, how it governs our thoughts and emotions, how it manifests during rebirth. We even discussed topics I hadn't given much thought to, such as the qi of the artificially created. People such as your friend Carl, here."

"Excuse me?" said Carl.

"It's something I hadn't considered before," said Gerrold to my pal. "Do androids have a qi? How does it manifest? Given my background, I had to defer to Valerie on her thoughts on the matter. I simply don't have much experience with your kind."

The heat must've been getting to me. Gerrold's idealistic, pseudo-religious arguments almost made sense.

Almost. "Taoism, rebirth, *qi*. Got it. So what drove you and Valerie apart?"

Gerrold shrugged. "Not sure. Like I said, perhaps she didn't find the answers she sought in our teachings."

"What makes you think that?" asked Carl.

"She started discussing other philosophies with me before she left," said Gerrold. "Buddhism, confucianism, candomblé. Plus all kinds of others. Weird ones I'd never heard of."

"Weirder than yours?" I snickered uncontrollably at my own humor, even though it didn't seem particularly funny.

Gerrold's eyes narrowed. "Yes."

"Did Valerie mention Veesnu by any chance?" asked Carl.

"She did," said Gerrold.

"Ah. So..." The words sounded loud in my own ears, and they felt momentous. Important. I couldn't put my finger on why, though. Possibly due to the acoustics of the sweat lodge.

Carl glanced at me before turning back to Gerrold. "Have you seen Valerie since she left those few months ago?"

Gerrold shook his head.

"Any chance you've been to the city recently?" asked Carl.

"Nope. Haven't left this camp in years. Don't have any reason or desire to."

"And I don't suppose you've ever heard of a place called Keelok's Funporium?"

Gerrold shook his head again. "Say...Valerie's ok, isn't she?"

"She's fine," said Carl. "She had a break-in at her place, that's all."

My tongue moved through molasses as I licked my lips, which felt inordinately dry despite the omnipresent steam. I laughed for some reason. "Hehe. Funporium..."

Carl turned to me. "Are you doing ok?"

"Me? I'm fine, dude. But could you tone it down? You're being extremely loud."

"I'm speaking at a normal volume." Carl glanced at Gerrold. "Do you use wood to heat this rock pit?"

I chuckled again. "Hehe. *Wood*."

"Yes. A mixture," said the dreadlock-laden naturalist. "Apple and mango from the orchards. Some mesquite. But we add a dash of something special to make the sweat lodge experience more relaxing. I was sure your friend would enjoy it once I heard about his family pedigree."

"You hotboxed the hut?" said Carl.

My droid pal was on fire. Nothing but zingers. "Hehe. Box."

"Wonderful." Carl shook his head in disbelief. "Can you help me get him dressed?"

"Sure," said Gerrold. "I suppose it's my fault for not warning you."

"Guys, I can walk," I said. "My legs are fine. They're just HUGE."

I looked down. Strangely enough, they were.

Gerrold and Carl helped me to my feet. We stumbled toward the door, and I wondered where in the world my clothes had gone.

Gremlins. Must've been gremlins, I thought.

From behind a fluffy cloud, Paige laughed at me. Or with me. I wasn't sure.

14

I popped a couple Buzzkill™ brand sobriety pills into my mouth as I swiped the pack across the pharmacy counter scanner. I followed it across the scanner's black maw with a tub of extra-strength antihistamine gel.

The counter squawked at me as I tried to finalize the order. "Would you like to add a tube of Benzitol to your order? Rated number one in customer satisfaction for burns, rashes, and bites. Or perhaps a pack of virility enhancers?"

I frowned and wondered what exactly the damn counter knew about me. "No. Paige, could you pay this dang thing and make it shut up?"

My Brain fairy silently obliged. I took my things and left.

On the sidewalk outside the pharmacy, I cracked open the tub of soothing gel and slathered a layer over my neck and arms. My skin prickled in response, but in a good way—the equivalent of eating ice cream for my sense of touch.

"Ah...that's better," I said.

Carl stood next to me, grinning. "So apparently co-pious amounts of sweating, mild smoke inhalation, and a tetrahydrocannabinol high aren't good remedies for bee stings."

I didn't take the smile as a slight. I knew Carl better than that. He was just glad I'd survived our harrowing trip to the country with nothing more than a few bumps and a headache—one that was rapidly disappearing thanks to the pills.

"Not so much," I said. "Although they're the perfect recipe for a wicked one-two punch of dry mouth and belly riots. I feel like I could eat an entire bison and guzzle roughly its same weight in water. Come on. Let's get some chow."

I prodded Paige for restaurant recommendations, preferably those specializing in juicy, charred meat patties served between buttery, toasted buns. My Brain mate suggested a burger joint a few blocks away called You, Me, and Umami. Feeling the need to stretch my legs after suffering through another pair of lengthy cab and tube rides, I suggested to Carl that we walk.

Tau Ceti sat low in the sky, probably not more than a sleep cycle and change away from the horizon. For the time being, though, it continued to do a stand-up job of roasting me with its rays.

"So, uh...did I miss anything back there?" I asked.

"At Gerrold's little slice of heaven?" asked Carl.

I nodded.

"You never blacked out, if that's what you mean," my partner said. "But I can't vouch for what you might've missed as a result of Mr. Stein's unique choice of incense."

"Mind filling me in? Paige's not much use to me at the moment."

I take offense to that, she said.

"You know what I mean." As useful as Paige was, she depended upon my body's sensory inputs for information. When hopped up on psychoactive drugs, the sensory streams in the organic portions of my mind tended to get crossed. For all intents and purposes, Paige had also been as high as a kite for the past couple hours.

Yes, but unlike you, I have Carl's feed of the events to go on, said Paige.

"Why don't you ask me what you're curious about," said Carl. "I don't know the precise moment you transformed from somewhat goofy Rich to drop your pants and run around screaming Rich."

"I did that?"

Carl shrugged. "To be fair, the pants were still damp. When they touched your skin, you claimed eels were trying to make love to your thighs, though you used a more crude turn of phrase."

I ran a hand across my face. "You've got to be kidding me."

"Nope. But it's alright. Several of the female members of the camp made positive remarks about the appearance of your legs. Apparently, you're very 'gazelle-like.'"

"Comes from years of kickboxing. The muscle tone doesn't go away easily." I sighed. "Oh, well. Not like I'm ever going back there. At least I put on a show, right?"

Carl nodded.

"So, back to Stein," I said.

"What about him?"

"Do you think he's involved?"

Carl shook his head. "No. He seemed genuine. Pupil dilation was normal—at least at first, before the effects of the cannabis smoke began to affect him. All signs point to him telling us the truth. The fact that his and Valerie's relationship ended recently seems to be circumstantial."

"And you don't have any reason to suspect he holds a grudge against Valerie?"

"To the point where he'd travel to the city, break into her apartment, and rifle through her things?" Carl gave his head another sharp shake. "No. And to what end? To get something back from Miss Meeks? The man has nothing worth taking, unless you're particularly fond of mangoes, honey, or marijuana."

"That's what I thought, but I was hoping you might've seen things differently." I wiped at my neck. The medicine had done its trick, but the hot sun combined with the residual layer of gel was making it sticky. "At least the trip wasn't a total wash. We learned Valerie's in the midst of a bicentennial, existential crisis, and she's trying to fill the void within her with mystical mumbo-jumbo of any flavor. It might explain her odd behavior earlier today. I've heard about strange cult practices before. Indoctrination. Some verge on brainwashing. Although, I have to admit—I'll be disappointed if you're wrong and Valerie is just a nutbag suffering from religious hallucinations."

Carl tilted his head and gave me a look. "Even nut-bags, as you call them, tend not to be lucid one moment and confused the next."

"I guess. Not without help, in any case."

We'd reached the restaurant. I found us an empty table. The menu flashed on the counter—scrolling images of grilled meats crowned with towers of cheese and toppings. Suggested pairings hovered underneath, most of them fried. I had Paige send in an order for the fattest, juiciest burger the joint offered as well as a tall glass of water, a pitcher of beer, and a jug of cola that would surely give me diabetes if I wasn't so genetically sheltered from the disease.

Carl seemed up for conversation, but between my lingering headache, the pack of rabid coyotes gnawing at my insides, and the lingering feeling of foolishness I felt over exposing myself to a clan of unBrained free spirits, I wasn't in the mood for much talking. Besides, I needed time to mull over my thoughts—most of which centered around Valerie and only a few of which involved her bulging chest and curvaceous hips.

What was her game, anyway? If she'd been lucid, why would she lie and pretend not to know us when we found her at the bakery? What was she covering up? And why would she seek us out in the first place if she didn't want us digging into her past?

The burger came and I feasted, filling my belly with savory mouthfuls that validated the place's namesake and washing it all down with alternating gulps of sweetened and fermented beverages. Once sated, I headed back to my place with Carl for some much needed shuteye, unfinished thoughts still swirling around my melon.

15

My head pounded, the melodic rhythm of my mind's inner drunken blacksmith taking his frustrations out on the beaten steel sides of my skull.

Thump. Thump. Thump.

I stuffed my head further under my pillows and hoped more sleep would solve the effects of my previous day's beverage choices.

Thump. Thump. Thump.

Are you going to get that? said Paige.

"Get what?" I mumbled.

The door, she said.

Thump. Thump. Thump.

Come to think of it, the thumping wasn't coming from inside my head. It was a sound—one I could hear with my actual ears and everything.

"Wait...are you saying someone's at the door?"

Ding, ding! said Paige. *We have a winner!*

I pulled my head from its synthetic down cocoon and glanced at the windows. Following my gaze, Paige undimmed them, revealing a mellow, natural light. Twilight wasn't more than a few hours away now.

"Why is someone here now?" I said.

Good question, said Paige. *You could ask.*

Thump. Thump. Thump. Thump.

"And why aren't they using the chime?"

Paige clicked her tongue at me electronically. *Another quality question. One I can't answer because I don't read minds. Except yours, of course.*

I pushed my feet off the side of my bed and lifted myself upright, my head swirling in response. Apparently, while the thumping was real, so too was my hangover. I grabbed a few more Buzzkills from the pack I'd laid at my bedside and chased them with a long draught from a glass and pitcher combo I'd left beside them. Then I sat and contemplated my existence while I worked on perfecting my blinking skills.

Thump. Thump. Thump. Thump. Thump.

Ooh. Five this time, said Paige. *Someone's getting antsy.*

I yawned, stood, and threw on a lamb's wool robe over my skivvies. "If this is a solicitor, I'm going to give them a piece of my mind. And where the hell is Carl? I got him for purposes such as this."

Technically you inherited him, said Paige.

I waved my hand in the air to dismiss her, despite the fact that she wasn't actually there in the room with me, and headed out of my bedroom. From there, I hooked a left down the hall onto my wrought iron, spiral staircase—a feature I'd added to give a touch of elegance to my place, since living in a three-story penthouse with an atrium and a sitting room wasn't ostentatious enough. I clattered down the steps two at a time as the Buzzkills took effect. I reached the front as another round of thumping began.

In a fit of impulsiveness and annoyance, I instructed Paige to flick the door open.

She did. It flicked. And I gaped.

Standing before me in tight paisley leggings and an egg yolk-colored halter top was none other than Valerie Meeks, her knuckles raised in mid-knock.

"Um...hi," she said.

I blinked a few more times, absorbing Valerie's curves and trying to make sense of the day. Although the Buzzkills had done their trick, they'd done nothing for my grogginess. I should've popped some stimulants, too.

I tried to muster the cream of my wit. I failed. "This is my apartment."

"I know," said Valerie.

"Why are you at my apartment?"

"Because you weren't at your office."

Her logic was unassailable. I was not at my office. "Fair enough. What I meant was, why are you here at all? My memory is a bit fuzzy thanks to a couple pitchers of fermented barley and hops and an all-expenses-paid trip to the land of the magic fairies courtesy of your ex-boyfriend, Gerrold, but I seem to remember you telling me to get lost yesterday."

Valerie wrung her hands, and her head shrunk back into her neck ever so slightly. I felt a twinge in my heart, despite the fact that I'd been the one on the receiving end of an epic tongue lashing mere hours prior.

"I know," said Valerie. "And I'm *really* sorry. Truly I am. I wish things could've gone differently, but the past is the past and what's done is done. Know that I never meant to hurt you."

"You have a funny way of showing it," I said.

She shrugged.

I blinked again. I felt like I was suffering through an epidemic of that particular bodily function. "So I'm guessing since you're here you remember who I am?"

Valerie nodded, her strawberry blond curls bouncing like cute little hair springs.

"You still haven't told me why you're here, you know," I said.

"I need you back on the case," she said.

I stood there, eyebrows furrowed, looking at her and not telling her that I hadn't actually quit on her case after she'd told me to do so.

Apparently, she took my silence as confusion. "As I said, I'm incredibly sorry about yesterday. People were watching. There were things that couldn't be said in public."

"Things?" I said. "What things?"

"Information. About the people involved in this case," said Valerie as she glanced over her shoulder furtively. "I wish I could say more, but in fairness to the people involved, I can't."

My brain hurt, similar to the way it used to the morning after a kickboxing bout. "Wait. Hold the horses for a second. Yesterday you came to me to get my help in investigating a break-in, something you claimed to have no knowledge about other than the fact that there was no record of anyone trespassing on your property. Then the evidence we found at your place—which was clearly planted by the way—sent me on a crazy trek ultimately leading nowhere, except when I got back your place had been tossed and you claimed not to know me. Now you're telling me that was an act, and there's people after you?"

"Yes, exactly! The Diraxi." Valerie looked over her shoulder again, as if she heard noises.

I leaned my head out the door and looked around. Val and her cute round tushy were the only ones in the hall. One of the benefits of the penthouse suite was not having to share the common areas with nosy neighbors.

"Are you sure you're doing ok?" I asked. "Do you want to come in and sit down?"

The elevator behind Valerie dinged, signaling the lift's arrival. I looked up in surprise, but Valerie nearly suffered a heart attack from shock. She emitted an un-ladylike squawk and bolted for the stairs.

"Hey! Wait!" I called, the folds of my robe flapping open as I took off after her. "Why are you running?"

She burst through the fire door and raced down the steps—at an alarming speed, I might add—calling to me as she ran. "I can't say more. Go to the bakery. Pass code twenty-seven, forty-nine. Second drawer, left of the stand mixer. Should explain things. Sorry!"

I stood at the head of the stairs for a moment, the stairwell breeze tickling my bare legs, before I remembered the elevator. I'm not sure who I expected, but Miss Crabbleman, my surly neighbor from downstairs, surely wasn't it.

"Lady problems?" she said.

"What do you want?" I asked. "This isn't your floor."

"I heard a thumping."

"Yes, we all did," I said. "There was someone at my door. *My* door. On *my* floor."

"I'm aware of that. But apparently you're unaware of the noise ordinances. If someone's causing a disturbance at your door, it's your responsibility to take care of it. You should be glad I didn't call the police. I'd be within my rights, you know."

"Yes, well, I've taken care of the problem, as it may be." I glanced back down the stairs. Valerie was long gone. I sighed and trudged back to my door.

Miss Crabbleman stood rooted in place.

"Well?" I said.

"Nice calves," she said, with a single raised eyebrow.

"Go away."

I went inside and closed the door. Carl stood within, apparently manning the gates to my castle.

"Where have you been?" I asked.

"I was recharging," he said with a shrug. "Why, what's going on?"

Let me, said Paige.

Carl tilted his head ever so slightly to the side, which was the usual look he gave while receiving an info-dump. "Ah. I see."

I shook my head. "I could've used backup you know. If you'd been here, I could've gone after Valerie and left you to deal with the sourpuss from downstairs."

"Well, pardon me for needing to refill my cells every few days. Even though it only takes me a half hour, whereas it takes you at least that long three times a day to fill the chemical digester you call a stomach. You know, this wouldn't be an issue if you approved of the compact fusion upgrade."

"Oh, don't start with me again," I said. "You know how I feel."

"I'm just saying," said Carl. "There's advantages. And no medical risks as determined from clinical trials."

"*Riiight,*" I said. "You know those trials are woefully short. Neutron damage is long term, my friend."

A trill sounded in the back of my mind, and my spirits momentarily soared. "Wait, hold on. I'm getting a call. Paige, is that Val?"

Sorry, sport, she said. *Looks like it's a GenBorn address.*

"GenBorn? What do they want?" I asked. "Patch them through."

Paige obliged.

"Hello Mr. Weed. This is a reminder of your appointment next week on Thursday, galactic standard date oh-seven, ten, thirty-three thirty at oh-nine hundred hours for your bi-annual rejuvenative services. Remember to arrive at least fifteen minutes before your scheduled appointment. Also remember not to eat any solids past oh-twenty-two hundred hours of the previous day, and no liquids are permitted—"

I had Paige silence the rest. I looked at Carl and shook my head.

"What?" he said.

"I can't believe you," I said. "Using a burdensome situation like the one I just labored through to push your pro-neutron agenda."

Carl sighed. "It's not an *agenda*. It's a mutually beneficial upgrade, for all the reasons I've already described."

"Whatever. You ready to make a trip out to a bakery?"

"Are *you?*" Carl eyed my soft, sleek robe.

"Admittedly, this wrap is rather breezy," I said. "I should probably change. Give me a minute."

16

The café doors zipped open as I stepped in front of them, admitting me to a den of soft, pillowy chairs, secluded reading and gaming nooks, and racks filled with assorted, low-priced knickknacks, all of them completely useless to the average coffee-swiller but nonetheless placed at prominent locations and advertised with flashy, lighted holosigns. A mellow soft rock tune hung over the establishment like a cloud of vanilla odor spray—inoffensive enough, but definitely there.

I walked to the counter where an overzealous barista bot greeted me.

"Welcome to StarGrinds, the galaxy's premier choice in coffee and coffee-related beverages. May I take your order?"

"Tall coffee. Black. Cream." I pinched my fingers a few millimeters apart to show how much.

If the bot had more expressive abilities than your average order-taking unit, it would've given me an odd look to signify what it thought of my request. I could've ordered a quadruple espresso mochaccino latte root beer float or something equally ludicrous, but since I didn't, it got to work on pouring out my uninspired beverage of choice. While it did so, I picked out the most delectable Danish—which wasn't saying much—from a pile below the counter and added it to my total. After a few moments, the bot handed me my cup of joe and I found a free table by the windows.

"You know how I know it's too early?" I asked Carl.

"How?" he asked as he sat down.

"Because we're at a coffee shop and we're the only ones here. Well, except for that guy." I pointed out a zoned-out gray-suited individual sitting at a window a few nooks down. "But he looks like he's been here all night—playing Brain games most likely. So technically, we're first."

"You know what they say about early risers?" said Carl.

I shook my head. "I'm not really in the mood for archaic agrarian proverbs right now."

I sipped my coffee and stared out the window. Across the street, Valerie's bakery sat there, closed, with the lights off—a little slice of simplicity in a modern sea of polymers, steel, and electromagnetism. The drapes hanging inside the windows reminded me of something out of a docuvid about humanity at the turn of the twentieth century. The entire building had a quaint, domestic feel about it. I suppose that was the logical marketing technique to adopt for a bakery, but the impression the building gave me was very different than the impression I'd come to generate about Valerie.

To be fair, the Valerie who'd introduced herself to me yesterday seemed a perfect match for the bakery: warm, caring, trusting, and, despite her appearance, fairly simple at heart. But the impression I'd crafted of the woman had taken a few unexpected turns since I'd first left her apartment building. For one thing, I was becoming more and more certain she'd been the one to plant the token from Keelok's Funporium in her own sock drawer, but the question was why? And that was only one of many questions I had regarding her behavior. Why did she lie about not knowing me yesterday in front of the bakery? She claimed the Diraxi were after her, but the only Diraxi I'd seen had been the pair at the Veesnu chapel. What possible reason would they have to come after her? They'd seemed like a fairly level-headed couple, after accounting for their alien eccentricities and choice of religious affiliations. Did she think they were spying on her? Why would they do that? And why would she fear it? What was she hiding that she didn't want others to know? And why involve me in it, of all people?

I snorted. Looking back, I never would've guessed the most sensible part of the previous day would've been my trip to Valerie's stoner ex-boyfriend's place. At first I'd wondered how he fit in, but the simplicity I'd seen at the heart of Valerie—the desire to craft and create something from nothing, the desire she'd told me about on our shared cab ride, the need that drove her to bake—all that fit with Gerrold. Despite his love of the chronic, he also seemed like a level guy, and more well-read and philosophical than I would've thought. He said he thought Valerie didn't find what she was looking for at his camp or from his personal religious and spiritual system, and that's what drove her away. So what was Valerie looking for? Whatever it was, it had led her to Gerrold, interested her in bizarre religions, gotten her mixed up with a pack of Diraxi, and driven her to me. What possible connection could exit between me and those other factors?

"Could you remind me what we're doing here, again?" asked Carl.

"We're here because I ran out of caffeine pills, and because I prefer the real deal to a tasteless, white oval," I said. "Besides, even if I did have any pills at home, I would've needed something to chase them with. What better than the warm, bitter, chocolate-colored concoction we call coffee."

Hah. I'll give you a warm, bitter, chocolate-colored concoction, said Paige.

It was a joke. Even though Paige was nothing more than a voice in my head and a few billion lines of code on a server, I'd always imagined her as having caramel-colored skin, spiky black hair, and bright green eyes—because, as a human, I had a need to anthropomorphize pretty much anything I came into contact with. Really. I was the kind of guy who found smiley faces in his toast and superheroes fighting demons in the clouds.

"That's not what I meant," said Carl. "Why are we sitting here when we could be at Valerie's place. She gave you the entry pass code."

"Yes, she did."

"So?"

"A couple reasons," I said. "One—the coffee, which I already explained. Two—I felt a need to sit and think for a while. A freak occurrence, yes, I know, but there you have it. And three—I was hungry, and we didn't have anything suitable at home. *Someone* never went grocery shopping last night."

"I meant to, but I needed to charge, and the vacuum bot required maintenance," said Carl. "I also didn't anticipate getting up so early."

"You're not the only one," I said. "Hence the *tall* coffee."

"I'll go to the store today. But, in the meantime..." Carl pointed out the window and tapped.

"I know," I said. "But I've only fulfilled two of the reasons for why we're here."

Before Carl could ask, I picked up the Danish and took a bite.

"How is it?" asked Carl.

"It's everything I've come to expect from a vast, multi-world conglomerate with over two hundred thousand locations like StarGrinds."

"So it's terrible."

"Awful," I said, dropping the pastry back onto my plastic dish.

"You know, I can think of a place that might have better pasties." Carl tapped on the window again.

"Trust me, the irony of eating breakfast at Star-Grinds when there's a perfectly serviceable bakery across the street isn't lost on me. But..."

"But what?" said Carl.

"Well, for one thing, I rather doubt Valerie's been in the bakery this morning. That place looks deader than an intros-only party. The pastries probably aren't fresh."

"And that freeze-dried yeast pocket is?" Carl pointed at my sorry excuse for a Danish.

"Point taken," I said.

"So what's point two?"

I shrugged, curling the corner of my lips and tilting my head to the side. "I'm not sure if our deal with Valerie is still valid."

"You mean your shrewdly-negotiated contract for five years worth of bear claws?"

"Yes."

"And you're concerned about taking unearned pastries without permission? Because you haven't completed the case yet?"

I nodded.

Carl raised an eyebrow. "When did you become so ethical?"

I snorted. "That's a low blow. I've always been ethical."

"You're going to need to provide examples," said Carl.

"Seriously?" I said. "I always floss before bed. I instruct Paige to open doors for ladies whenever I'm on dates. And I never once intentionally kicked an opponent in the groin during any of my kickboxing bouts."

Carl smiled. "I'm not sure you understand the meaning of that word, but you can relax. I'm messing with you."

I furrowed my brows. "Better add a trip to the RAAI Corp factory next to the grocery store on your to-do list. Seriously, that firmware update did things to you, my friend."

"Look, Valerie explicitly said you were back on the case this morning, right?"

"Yes."

"Then it's ethical to take an advance on your bear claw bounty, such as it may be," said Carl. "Ask Paige if you doubt me."

Paige didn't wait for my input. *Go ahead. Stuff your face.*

"Alright, fine. You've talked me into it," I said. "And after this, we can also add gambling and prostitution next to grocery shopping on your to-do list."

I think Carl got the joke, but his facial expressions were so hard to read sometimes. His current one lingered somewhere between mirth and longing. It could've been due to my comment, but then again, maybe he wanted to stuff his face with bear claws and didn't want to bother with emptying his catch chamber.

17

Carl and I walked across the street to the bakery. Paige relayed Valerie's pass code to the shop's doors, which slid apart soundlessly, and lights flickered on as we walked into the establishment.

The front of the house was more or less what I'd expected after gazing, moon-eyed, at the exterior. Dainty round ivory tables lounged to my left and right, each paired with a duo of white enameled wrought iron chairs that promised to make the act of sitting about as fun as sex during the Victorian era. Each table held a vase hand-picked from a different rummage sale, but all held a selection of a half dozen white lilies and sunflowers—fake, most likely, though it was difficult to tell with the modern, ever-bud varietals some nurseries sold.

At the counter, pastel yellow and white streamers hung from the front in neat, evenly-spaced crescents, partly disguising a display half-filled with the remains of yesterday's efforts—but what a yield of efforts it was.

Chocolate éclairs, raspberry Danishes, and cinnamon chip scones hung out in piles next to stacks of glazed fritters and profiteroles bursting with cream and dusted with powdered sugar. Their sticky, sugary smell filled my nostrils, along with a delicate almond scent that drifted my way from a rack of marzipan bars. At the bottom of the display, relegated to a corner as if some sort of second-class, yeast-raised citizen, sat the objects of my affection.

"Ah, there they are," I said.

I walked around to the back of the display, jiggered open the back panel, and snagged a bear claw. With its sugary glaze seeping over my fingers, I parted my lips and sunk my teeth into the nut-crusted delight. Flavors exploded over my tongue as pastry met flesh. I closed my eyes and savored the experience as I chewed.

When I reopened my eyes, I found Carl staring at me with ill-concealed envy.

I swallowed. "Dude, seriously. Indulge yourself. These are worth it."

He held up a hand. "It's ok. I'm fine."

I wolfed down another bite. "I'm not kidding. These are amazing. Valerie can *cook*. Who knew?"

"It's not that I don't trust you," said Carl. "It's that...how should I put this? Sometimes I wonder if I truly have all the same senses as you. Because watching you dive into that pastry and seeing the look on your face as its flavors reached the pleasure centers of your brain...well, it doesn't happen that way with me."

I ate the rest of the thing in three bites, then sucked my fingers to get the last bits of glaze. "Well, I can't comment on that, old friend. But if you're right, we need to petition RAAI Corp for them to come out with a firmware update for *that* instead of your personality. Missing out on these babies is a crime."

"I think we'd need a hardware update instead," said Carl.

"You have my approval for it," I said. "But don't get any ideas. No springing for a neutron cannon while it's being installed."

Carl rolled his eyes. I grabbed a second bear claw and waltzed around to the back.

I nearly tripped over a wet vac bot. It whirred over the floor like a mechanical slug, leaving a trail of wet suds behind it as it sucked up dirt, water, and soap through a vacuum nozzle. As soon as it sensed me, its gears clicked and it surged forward, desperate to suck up the soapy scum at my feet so I wouldn't slip.

Behind it, a rudimentary all-purpose droid scrubbed an ivory marble countertop. It was a model that didn't even feature flesh-like prosthetics, but why would it? Like all cleaning units, it would be programmed to function while people were away. As soon as it spotted us, it zipped into a slim alcove, a door winking shut behind it to hide it. Apparently, dirty counters didn't pose the same safety hazard wet floors did.

As the vacuum bot finished its work, I took a moment to examine the kitchen and consume the rest of my second almond-coated pastry. A pair of hulking stone hearth deck ovens dominated the center of the space, making the broad, stainless steel prep tables on either side look frail by comparison. The marble countertop ran around the entire perimeter of the room, its surface cluttered with mixers and sheeters and bowls of all sizes. A white subway tile backsplash met the counter at a neat ninety degree angle, and knickknacks and bric-a-brac hung from studs high up on the walls, out of reach of flour and grubby fingers. Every color of a bride's rainbow was represented, from snow to seashell to cornsilk. I wondered how Valerie could stand it, given her marital status.

The vacuum bot slurped a final bit of liquid off the floor and zoomed off. Carl glanced at me sideways as it did so. "So...second drawer, left of the stand mixer?"

"You got the full feed from Paige," I said. "You remember better than me."

"Yes. Right. It's just that, well..." He pointed.

By my count, there were a full dozen mixers lined up along the wall.

I sighed. "Figures. Well, you know the drill. Start digging."

"And what exactly are we looking for?" asked Carl.

"We're working on the same parameters we had at Valerie's place."

"So we have absolutely no clue," said Carl.

"Right."

I picked a cabinet on one end of the mixer conga line and Carl started at the other end. My first foray into the drawers yielded an assortment of whisks and basting brushes as well as one extremely long handled wooden spoon.

"You know, if I were human," said Carl, "I believe I'd be experiencing a sensation of déjà vu."

"Huh?" I said. "You dig through the kitchen while I'm sleeping?"

"I simply meant this situation is remarkably similar to our first, undirected search at Miss Meeks' place."

"If you're insinuating Valerie's the puppet master behind Keelok's game token, I'm way ahead of you. The question is why."

My next two drawers contained a selection of piping tips and bags as well as a number of offset spatulas.

"I wonder if perhaps Miss Meeks' initial visit to us wasn't driven by her break-in, such at it might've been, but something else," said Carl.

I turned a cookie scoop over in my hand. "Huh? Like what?"

"Perhaps Miss Meeks' actions were a cry for help."

"You know there's hotlines for that sort of thing," I said.

"Not what I meant," said Carl. "I don't think she's suicidal. I'm wondering if she had a problem only *we* can solve."

I was having a hard time processing my friend's line of thought. "But...she did come to us. To solve a problem."

"Never mind," said Carl. "It's an unfounded assumption. The facts are too scant to draw any conclusions."

I pulled open another drawer. Tucked away at the bottom, a mostly transparent slip caught my eye.

"Hey, check this out." I pulled out the slip and held it to the light. In the middle of the card, my eyes found a familiar image—a neuron superimposed over a beaming, white-hot sun.

"Another Veesnu cardslip," said Carl, walking over.

I tapped the slip against my chin in thought. "So, Valerie did send us to the spaceport, but why do so in such a roundabout fashion? And why does she want us to go up there again? What's so special about that chapel, other than those delectable waffles?"

Nice try, hotshot, but you're a little off, said Paige. *I blocked the obligatory Veesnu bible from downloading to your Brain, but check out what else is on there.*

As before, a translucent hologram filled my field of vision upon Paige's activation of the slip. The same shiny Dirax, complete with crossing teal and navy sashes on its carapace, stood in front of a burning star while floating, neuron-like blobs swirled above and below and behind. The alien spread its pincers and delivered the same subvocal spiel as before. As it prated on about the One Knowledge and Truth and the Ascension, I wondered why in the world Paige was making me sit through the sermon again.

Wait for it, she said.

If she hadn't warned me to be on the lookout, I would've missed it. At the conclusion of its speech, the address at the bottom of the hologram was different. This time it read: 13479 Rue de Camp, Knottington, Pylon Alpha.

The hologram cut out. I tsked and shook my head. "Why are the pretty ones always liars?"

Carl tilted his head and furrowed his eyebrows. "Excuse me?"

"Valerie. She said this would explain things." I held up the slip. "But I'm as confused as ever."

"Well, if I had to hazard a guess, I'd say the Veesnu religion plays a part in this somehow."

"It's keen deductive insights like that that keep you off silverware polishing detail," I said with a raised eyebrow. "But why is Valerie pointing us to a new chapel in Knottington, of all places? That's over in the industrial park near the RAAI Corp manufactory and the local GenBorn headquarters. I get that Valerie's looking for something, some meaning or purpose in her life besides what she derives from baking, but couldn't she have found it in a chapel nearer to her house?"

Not necessarily, said Paige. *A quick check shows only five Veesnu chapels in and around Pylon Alpha, including the one on the spaceport. There's one slightly closer than the Knottington location, but not by much. It's a difference of perhaps five minutes, given typical traffic conditions.*

"I meant you can get your fill of crazy in a wide flavor of religions," I said. "What makes Veesnu so special?"

You want the short version or the long version? asked Paige.

"It was more of a rhetorical question," I said. "If I cared that much, I'd read their bible."

"That could be a useful activity, you know," said Carl, "seeing as this is the second time the religion has reared its head in our case."

I grimaced. "Um, yeah. I have a hard enough time getting through boring novels. You think I'll make it through a Veesnu bible without falling asleep two minutes in?"

"On the other hand, I hear Knottington is lovely this time of year," said Carl.

I smiled. "Now you're talking my language. Let's go."

18

Despite my protests, Paige attempted to give me a crash course in Veesnu during our tube trip and subsequent cab ride, but my brain simply wasn't attuned to the religion's esoteric doctrines. After the third stripped-down explanation of the Ascension, its basis in Diraxi culture, and its possible metaphysical connotations, Paige and I agreed it might be better for me to approach the next stop in our liquor-free bar crawl with an open mind. So I spent the rest of the trip deep in thought—or at least as deep as I could get with the ever-present temptation of Brain games.

After a few games of Smashblocks in which I barely scored a billion points, I called it quits. My mind wasn't in it. Carl, gazing out the cab window with a vacant stare, looked how I felt.

"Still thinking about Valerie's motivations?" I asked.

He turned his eyes to the cab interior. "Yes. Among other things."

"Such as?"

"The other parties involved in this situation," he said. "As much as Valerie's wishes and motivations concern me—and I do believe those, more than anything, are at the heart of our case—we can't ignore that, even if she set us up during her initial exposé, someone else is involved. She didn't toss her own apartment into a state of disarray. I'm increasingly sure of that."

I wanted to add a clever insight to Carl's musings, but I didn't have any, so I kept my mouth shut and cast my eyes to the skies. Tau Ceti hovered at the horizon, painting the heavens in lovely shades of plum, ginger and lemon. Above and to the east, the solar reflectors caught the fading rays of sunshine, winking into existence like a slew of small moons evenly spaced throughout the sky.

Our cab zipped onto False Cross before merging onto Rue de Camp. As the street numbers ticked north, condo high-rises gave way to sprawling manufacturing complexes, including the two-kilometer long local fabrication arm of RAAI Corp's droid business. Eventually, as we approached a small strip mall populated by burrito joints and ethnic alien eateries, our cab slid to a halt.

The Veesnu chapel, though substantially larger than the one we'd visited at the spaceport, wasn't particularly church-like. No tall spires or turrets graced its rooftop. No elaborate carvings hand-chiseled by a child prodigy faced the street, nor did holoprojectors stream vids of revivals into the air above. If anything, the building resembled an oversized shipping container, and it sparkled with roughly the same amount of artistic flair. I wouldn't have recognized it if not for the projected sign featuring the now-familiar sun and neuron combination that hovered over the front.

"So, what's our play?" asked Carl as we exited the cab.

"What do you mean?" I said. "I figured I'd walk in and ask about Val."

Carl emitted a soft humming sound and curled his lips.

"Bad idea?" I said.

"What if they're involved in the case? Miss Meeks claimed Diraxi were after her. Being direct could divulge more information than we want."

I sucked on my lips and nodded. "Hm. Good thinking. Alright, new plan. You go in."

"Me?"

"No, the other Carl. Yes, you. Go in and ask about Valerie."

"I'm not sure you understand the crux of my argument," said Carl. "That'll still tip them off."

"It'll tip them off about *you*," I said, "but not about me. If they tighten their lips, I'll wait a while and follow you in with a new gambit."

Because of his base layer of programming predisposing him to being compassionate toward humans, Carl rarely looked surly, but this time he got pretty close. He turned and stomped into the building.

I glanced at the strip mall while I waited for Carl to return. The burrito joint I'd spotted was a chain affair, an Arabic-Mexican combo franchise by the name of Hallal-peños. Next to it stood an Asian-Tak fusion restaurant, which I assumed was a vegetarian place based on the traditional Tak diet of roughage, roughage, and more roughage. I even spotted a Diraxi place by the name of Hive Mind, Body, and Soul. I couldn't help but wonder what sort of hellacious mix of grubs and protein strands graced the establishment's menu—but then again, maybe the place just served waffles.

I played with my fingernails as I waited. "Paige, how's Carl doing?"

You want the live feed, or the condensed version? she asked.

"Option two please," I said. "Seeing life through someone else's eyes tends to bring on a sensation of vertigo. And sometimes vomiting."

Very well, my digital gatekeeper said. *There's a chaplain manning the front of the house. Carl asked about your enchanting lady friend with the memory problems. The chaplain said he didn't know anything about that.*

I grunted. "Is that it?"

Do you remember what I told you about the Ascension?

"Remember? Yes," I said. "Understand? No."

Well the chaplain is giving Carl a spiel about the process, and informing him that since he bypassed the organic Synthesis, he's ineligible for salvation. He's an affront to nature.

"And Carl's just standing there taking it?" I asked.

It's Carl. Of course he is, said Paige. *But he has his reasons. He's trying to keep the guy talking, hoping something useful might transmit out of his antennae.*

I twiddled my thumbs and chewed on my lip. It wasn't long until my sharp-featured inorganic pal returned.

"You're looking haggard," I said.

Carl glanced at his outfit. "I am?"

"It's an expression. Paige filled me in. How are you holding up?"

Carl shrugged. "The universe is full of bigots. Some of them happen to be overflowing with religious zeal. It's nothing new to me."

"You take it better than I would, that's for sure," I said. "If someone told me I was an affront to the gods, I might show them the prodigious ass-kicking skills *my* gods graced me with."

Carl snorted and smiled. "Perhaps it's best I went in first, after all."

"So, get anything useful?" I asked.

"Depends. How interested are you in the Ascension?"

I waved Carl off. "I have a feeling I'm going to be exposed to that myself soon enough. I don't need it from you, too. Why don't you drag yourself over to one of those eateries at the mall while I take my turn at the chaplain?"

"You have a plan?" asked Carl.

"Of course I do. Paige'll stream you the action as I go." I turned to head into the cube-shaped place of worship.

"You can always ping me if you need any help," said Carl.

I paused in mid-step. "I know."

"Don't do anything stupid, Rich."

I set my gaze on Carl and adopted my best stern matron face.

"Just thought it needed to be said, that's all." With more than a little hesitation, he headed off toward the outdoor mall.

I entered the chapel and found myself in a cylindrical entryway that felt tight at the shoulders. Any smaller and I might be able to throw a hook with my left elbow and hit myself in the right temple. A Dirax—tall, shiny, and dark, wearing a pair of criss-crossed sashes across its carapace—stood at a makeshift podium in front of a trio of hallways.

Welcome, Pilgrim, the thoughts appeared in my mind. *Bask in the splendor of Veesnu. How can I assist?* The Dirax spread its pincer arms in supplication.

Splendor? If the entryway were any more austere, they'd have to strip the walls off, but I kept my mouth shut. Insulting the Dirax's digs wouldn't help ingratiate me with him. Instead, I played the part of a dumb mark.

"Hi. I'm, uh...Rich. This is a church, right? Veesnu, it's called?"

Your language is imprecise, human, but not fully incorrect. We are practitioners of the One Truth, Veesnu. This structure is physical rather than metaphysical, but it is our conduit to the Knowledge and the Ascension, our Portal to Truth. Welcome.

"Um, thanks," I said as I scratched my neck. "Look, I'm...not sure why I'm here, to be honest. I've just...been going through some things, lately. And I'm a little confused, you know? Like about—"

Existence? Purpose? Motive? You seek Knowledge. You seek the One Truth.

"Well, I don't know about the last part, but yeah. There's a friend of mine who was going through similar emotions. They gave me this." I pulled out the card-slip. "So I figured, why not? I'd come see what you guys had to offer."

The Dirax spread its pincer arms out even farther and tucked in its head. *Veesnu envelops you, Pilgrim. The One Truth awaits. Although your friend's temporal sense is not yet fully aligned with the cosmos.*

"Excuse me?"

One of our sermons recently began. You are late. But I suppose I could let you join it in progress. Please, come with me.

The Dirax turned and walked off down the hallway behind it. I glanced into the halls to my left and right as I followed. The left contained nothing of note—just a few closed doors and a whole lot of empty space—but farther down the right hallway I spotted a bald, glassy-eyed male human, roughly my height, in a flowing navy blue robe. He glanced vacantly in my direction before disappearing into a doorway.

The Dirax stopped in front of a lift. It flicked its antennae and the down signal lit up. I waited patiently at its side.

"So your chapel is downstairs?" I asked.

The Dirax clicked its pincers. *I do not understand the query. The cosmos enfolds us, surrounds us. The practice of Veesnu is not spatially dependant.*

"Sorry. I simply meant, if your place of worship is below ground, what's the rest of this place for?"

Rooms for study. Contemplation. Quarters for us, and the disciples. Space to manifest the Ascension.

"Disciples?" I asked.

Practitioners of Veesnu. Seekers of the One Truth. Those whose journey into the metaphysical has brought them close to the Ascension.

"Like that guy in the navy robe I saw as we walked in?"

Correct.

The lift dinged, and the doors slid open with a puff. I entered the elevator, keenly aware of the Dirax's size.

"And, um, this ascension you keep talking about... What's involved in that?"

It is a journey of the mind. A physical, spiritual, and psychological test, one meant to free the psyche from the limits of the self and enter the ultimate, timeless expanse of the cosmos.

Sounds like a blast, huh? said Paige.

I ignored her. "And is this difficult?"

Extremely.

The lift stopped and the door opened. The Dirax held out a pincer. We exited and I followed the insectoid creature down a dimly lit hall to a closed door, which flicked open halfway as we approached. Darkness within loomed, thick and dense.

The sermon has begun. Enter, Pilgrim, and welcome Veesnu. Use senses beyond the visual. Absorb, do not emit. And bring to a forefront in your mind the will to accept.

I paused at the door, staring into the darkness, unfamiliar sounds leaking through the crack, and I started to question my plan. What the heck kind of sermon was this?

You've come this far, said Paige. *Might as well go through with it. Don't worry. I'll be here.*

I slipped into the room.

I blinked, trying to adjust my eyes to the gloom, but I could barely see. Diraxi voices bounced around my head, different streams of thought coming at once, as if multiple Diraxi were shouting and whispering and jabbering at me simultaneously.

The portrait of the cosmos stretches into infinity. Why must we accept an infinitesimal slice? Yearning is acceptance of the One Truth.

Using my hands, I fumbled forward until I found a seat. I took advantage of everything it had to offer, plopping myself into its cool embrace. Darkness swirled around me, sinking into the space between my eyelids, but there was a hint of light as well. No burning sun, just pale, floating specks.

Thought is concrete. A measure of the mind. Electrical pulses, transferred by neurons. All life, not merely human, or Diraxi, functions in such a manner.

Sounds rippled through the air, incoherent, indistinct, barely more than background noise. A slow, burning star—the voice of the cosmos, translated from electromagnetic impulses to pressure waves for human ears. Mist floated on my tongue, and my nose detected a clean, rich scent that reminded me of apples and rain.

Differences in composition, mental and physical, do not impede the metaphysical. They merely interfere with the process. The One Truth remains. The journey remains. The Ascension.

Something furry and foreign tickled my gut. I suppressed the urge to scream. The Dirax had instructed me to absorb, not emit. I think screams were included. But my gut defiantly felt odd. Was I hungry? The bear claws hadn't travelled through my esophagus that long ago.

The intensity of light in the room shifted, shocking my system. I floated in my chair, alone, before a blazing white sun as blobby neurons floated around me.

Good effects, I thought. *I can't even see the rest of the room. Or the floor. Or anyone else for that matter.*

I expected a snarky response from Paige but received precisely nothing. The smell of apples and rain intensified—which was odd, because I was floating in space—and I suppressed a sudden urge to vomit. Maybe the bear claws had been a bad idea.

I licked my lips, which felt exceedingly dry. Then I realized my lips didn't exist. Neither did my body.

Odd. Very odd, indeed, I thought.

I floated through the heart of the cosmos, the universe around me darkening as I contemplated where my lips had gone.

19

I wriggled my lips. They were back. So was my nose. The scent of apples and rain was gone, however. It had been replaced with something far less pleasant—urine and garbage, if I wasn't mistaken. Not a particularly effective scent for converting people to a religion, I had to say. And I'd also acquired a blinding headache, one that pounded on the inside of my skull like a gorilla given free reign with a felt-covered mallet.

This is even worse than that weedache I got from Gerrold's place, I thought.

Rich? Rich, is that you? Paige's familiar voice partially displaced the gorilla's drum solo.

"Hey. You're back," I said, the words slow and heavy on my tongue. "Where'd you go?"

Where'd I go? said Paige. *Where the heck did you go?*

"What do you mean?" I asked. "I'm at the Veesnu placeamabob. Chapel. Church. Whatever."

You want to double check that math, sport?

I cracked an eyelid and immediately regretted it. Blinding light filled my field of vision—except it didn't. The light was on the dim side. Diffuse, even. But it took me a moment to realize it. Apparently my brain still hadn't adjusted from the misty blackness of the sermon room.

I inched my eyelids open millimeter by millimeter. I spotted a couple unremarkable bricks walls, one of which I'd apparently befriended. I'd propped myself upright in the corner between it and a dumpster—which explained the smell.

"Where am I?" I asked.

In the alley behind Hallal-peños, said Paige. *A couple blocks from the chapel.*

"What happened to the apples? And the rain? And the vast expanse of the cosmos?"

Ex-squeeze me?

I couldn't recall Paige ever being stumped. Apparently there was a first time for everything. I squeezed my eyes back shut as I tried to think. "Sorry. What I meant was, how did I get here?"

I was hoping you could tell me, Paige said. *You went off grid for a while.*

"I did?"

Yup. Your Brain feed was acting completely normal. I could sense the sermon room, with the ambient music and the Diraxi preachers. You were there for a while, sitting and listening. And then—poof—your feed cut out. I couldn't even geolocate you. You popped back into existence in this alley. Those thoughts about your headache and Gerrold were the first transmission I got from you since you disappeared.

"Huh..." I said. "So you didn't see the burning star, or the blobby neurons, or the vast expanse of outer space? Or me losing my lips?"

No... said Paige. *Are you feeling alright?*

"Sure. Like a herd of Glieseian wildebeests trampled me. But they did so gently. How long was I out?"

About two hours, said Paige.

"Rich? Rich!"

Carl's voice echoed between the walls and into my ears. I cracked open my eyes and spotted my old pal near where the alley spilled into the street.

"Over here, bud," I called. "Where've you been?"

"At the ethnic Diraxi cuisine place, like you told me to," he said as he jogged over.

"How were the waffles?" I asked.

"Quit joking around," he said. "Are you ok?"

"Peachy," I said. "Now help me up. I'm not sure if my legs work."

"I'm hoping that's another joke." Carl leaned down and lifted me to my feet.

"It is." I thought. My knees wobbled as I put weight on them. "Didn't Paige fill you in on what happened?"

"As best she could, but that's not saying much."

"You going to take that from him?" I asked my Brain secretary.

It's not a jab, said Paige. *For once, I really don't know what happened. And your sensory feed is still garbled.*

My head throbbed and my knees felt weak. "You're not kidding, sister. Be glad you don't have to walk in my shoes."

Carl put his arm around my torso and helped me toward the street. "You think we should report this to the police?"

"And tell them what?" I asked. "That I woke up disordered and reeking of urine in an alley? I'm sure they'll believe me when I tell them I have no clue what happened, but I'm certain the nice priests over at the local church did it to me. The lingering drugs in my system will undoubtedly clinch their support."

"So what do we do?" asked Carl.

"What is this? A date? Do I have to make all the decisions?"

Carl looked at me, his face drawn, the concern clear in his eyes. It was a subtle display of emotion, one I hadn't expected out of him—the display, not the emotion itself. Perhaps he'd gotten an upgrade on his facial systems at some point along the line.

I sighed. "Look, I'm sorry. I'm just... I need to rest a little. Sit down. Why don't you call us a cab?"

Paige took charge of that. I leaned against Carl as we waited. The occasional whistle of a full cab zipping by broke the monotonous, low hum of the holoprojectors coming from the strip mall. Over by the Asian-Tak fusion place, an over-served patron made racy catcalls at passersby.

"I told you to be careful," said Carl in a quiet voice.

"You told me not to do anything stupid," I corrected. "It's not exactly the same thing."

"You know what I meant."

We let the hum of civilization wash over us, serenading us with its omnipresence. Honks, horns, whistles and music, speech and footfalls, all laid over an ever-present energetic *vibration* that filled every nook and cranny of populated space. I rarely noticed it. I blamed the allure of mobile Brain entertainment.

Soon enough, a cab pulled over and opened its doors.

"I'm assuming we're heading home," said Carl.

I nodded and sunk into the cool, air-conditioned surface of the back bench seat. My headache was improving, but not as fast as I'd hoped. The thin walls of the cab shut out the street noise, but they couldn't do anything to quiet the rhythmic, pulsing rush of blood through my ears.

"Did you bring any of those Buzzkills with you?" I asked as I felt the cab pull away.

Carl shook his head. "Want to head to a pharmacy?"

"I can wait until we get home."

Carl kept his eyes on me, still concerned. "Do you think they drugged you?"

I shrugged. "Not sure. My headache is similar to the one I had yesterday after Gerrold's all-natural aromatherapy treatment, but it's not exactly the same. It's more localized, way at the back of my skull. Feels like someone's trying to tunnel through."

I closed my eyes again and tried to block out the pounding. I needed to focus, to think—and to remember. What exactly had happened to me? One moment I'd been enjoying the subvocal syncopated stylings of a clerical Diraxi quartet, and the next I'd been floating, incorporeal, huffing apple fumes. Somewhere along there I'd gone missing and helped myself to all the best that a trash-filled alley had to offer. Did the Diraxi dump me there, or did I find my way to the dumpster myself? And did I do anything else while I'd been unconscious? Paige said I'd been out for roughly two hours.

"I think Valerie's behavior is finally starting to make sense," I said.

"Excuse me?" said Carl.

I opened my eyes. "We assumed Valerie was lying when she said she had no idea who we were outside her bakery. But you presented two likely scenarios with regards to her behavior that day."

"Yes," said Carl. "Either she was lying, or she didn't remember us."

"Right. I don't remember what I've been up to or where I've been for the past couple hours. Maybe I was in a coma, sitting pretty at the Veesnu chapel, getting indoctrinated, or perhaps I was out causing trouble. We don't know because I went off grid, according to Paige. It's pretty clear Valerie's in knee deep with these Veesnu chaps. Who's to say when she came to hire us, she wasn't suffering the same sort of swoon I just did?"

Carl steepled his fingers and rubbed them against the bottom of his chin. "So you're suggesting Miss Meeks wasn't aware of her actions when she first arrived at our office yesterday? That she was under the effects of some sort of Veesnu brainwashing? And that's why she behaved the way she did at her bakery?"

I nodded.

Carl drew his index finger and thumb across the top of his lips, down the sides of his mouth, and under his chin. He kept them there for a moment before shaking his head. "I'm not buying it."

"Huh?" I said. "Why not?"

"We've interacted with Miss Meeks three times now," said Carl. "Well, you have. I was charging during the third encounter. But I have Paige's feed of the incident. And Miss Meeks' behavior was consistent during two of the encounters. The only anomalous one occurred outside her bakery."

"Well, maybe that's when she was suffering a walking coma," I said.

"And in her bewildered state, she decided to do some baking?"

"That makes more sense than her seeking me out and bartering for my services while in the same condition." I leaned forward in my seat. "Look, back up and bear with me for a second. We're in agreement Valerie planted the initial piece of evidence in her apartment, right? The token from the arcade?"

"It's the most likely explanation," said Carl. "Especially considering her behavior this morning, where she pointed you in the direction of the Veesnu cardslip at her bakery."

"Right. Which means she's the one who directed us toward Keelok's Funporium, and the Veesnu chapel in the spaceport, and Fran's office at Cetie U. Each one of those stops was supposed to be a clue toward something. What the Veesnu chapel implied is obvious—the others less so. But Fran's a professor of exoneurobiology, specializing in Diraxi brain function. Remember how she said Veesnu is part religion and part science? Maybe Valerie's been trying to tell us what you so jokingly alluded to. Maybe the Diraxi have made strides in cross-species communication methods. Maybe the Diraxi *are* brainwashing people, and one of those people is Valerie."

"And where does Keelok's Funporium fit into all of this?" asked Carl.

I shrugged. "No idea."

Carl furrowed his brows and tilted his head. "Ok. Let's say you're right, or at least in the general ballpark. Here's a question for you: why go to the trouble of planting clues in the forms of arcade tokens and cardslips? Valerie sought us out. Why not simply ask for help? And why lie about the whole thing?"

"I don't know," I said. "But if she's being brainwashed, maybe she's suffering a mental blockage that prevents her from saying. Or maybe she left *herself* the clues during one of her out-of-body Veesnu experiences. Perhaps she's unaware of what the Diraxi are doing to her, but there's a part of her mind, a subliminal element, that's pushing her to search for answers. Maybe that part or her mind left the arcade token in the sock, hoping the lucid portion of her mind would find it and discover the truth."

"Those are interesting theories," said Carl, "but unfortunately, neither of them make sense. If Miss Meeks were suffering a mental block preventing her from telling others about what was befalling her at the hands of the Veesnu, then how is it she came to you earlier today and pointed you in the direction of the cardslip at her bakery? Similarly, if she was only aware of the Veesnu Diraxi's actions at a subliminal level, how was she able to come to you this morning and tell you the information she did?"

I leaned back into the cab cushions. Carl had a point. None of my theories fully accounted for our varied interactions with Valerie. Nonetheless, there had to be a scenario that explained both Valerie's selective memory and her inability to directly tell us what was happening to her, and my gut told me the Diraxi and their mind-bending, pseudo-religious Veesnu hypnosis sessions were behind it.

"Rich," said Carl. "Did you by any chance tell the Veesnu chaplain anything that could've tipped him off regarding your true motives for attending his sermon, or said anything that could've tied you to Miss Meeks?"

I shook my head. "Don't think so. I asked a few questions about Veesnu and the chapel, that's all. Why? What does that have to do with Valerie and her actions?"

"Nothing," said Carl, as he stared out the window at my back. "But it could have everything to do with why we're being followed."

20

"Say what?" I turned around and looked out onto the wide expanse of pavement behind us.

"The silver Feltberry crossover," said Carl. "Two cars back from us."

I spotted it. "It's following us?"

"Either that, or it happens to be travelling to the same tube station we are. I noticed it about a minute after we entered the cab."

"Well, let's test your theory, shall we?" I said. "Paige, instruct our car to make a detour. Let's take the next right, then the second left, then the first right again."

You got it, said Paige. *But don't blame me if the car throws a fit. You know how much these things hate being rerouted into less efficient traffic patterns.*

I snorted. As impressive an achievement as it was to have the entire surface of Cetie covered in interconnected, cross-communicating cabs loaded with visual and geopositional sensors, all humming along smoothly, driven by slick algorithms perfected over centuries, each individual car was dumber than dirt. One couldn't even order you a pizza if you'd asked it to. But I suppose it was natural for Paige to empathize with them. From a developmental standpoint, she had more in common with the fleet of cabs than she did with me.

Despite her protests, Paige sent the message. We turned—first to the right, then the left, then right again. I kept my eyes trained on the crossover the entire time. It followed us seamlessly.

I turned to Carl, wondering what a pain it must've been to tail someone back in the bygone days of yore when cars didn't drive themselves. "Well, that settles that. We're being followed." I smiled.

"And this amuses you?" asked Carl.

"Are you kidding?" I said. "Of course it does. It's different. It's exciting. This is the kind of stuff I signed up for when I established my investigation business a year ago."

"Kind of like waking up in a pile of trash in an alley?"

"You know, in those old novels and vids that inspired me to try my hand at detective work, people were always waking up unconscious in alleys after taking blows to the head. Perhaps that's a crucial aspect of the profession I overlooked."

Carl ignored my wisecrack. "What do you think we should do?"

"Figure out who's tailing us, obviously," I said as our cab took another left, trying to return us to the main thoroughfare.

"It's fairly obvious *who* it is," said Carl. "*Why* they're following us, assuming you didn't mention Miss Meeks while at the Veesnu chapel, is far more interesting."

I waggled a finger at my partner. "Don't assume anything. For all we know it's Fran or Keelok or even Valerie herself in that cab. Given how this case has unfolded, none of those alternatives would surprise me. Well, Keelok would. But mostly because I don't think he'd fit very well in the cab." I glanced out the back window again, spotting the crossover as it followed us around the corner. "Why don't we flip the script?"

"You mean follow whoever's following us?"

"Exactly."

Carl looked at me, his lips pressed together and his eyebrows elevated a hair above sea level.

"I can see you're not convinced, but bear with me." I glanced out the cab window. Glossy skyscrapers blotted out much of the light from the solar reflectors, the tall sentinels having replaced Knottington's sprawling manufactories as our cab worked its way closer to Pylon Alpha proper. "Paige, are there any large public gatherings nearby? Anywhere we might find crowds of people and aliens with which to mingle?"

At this hour? said Paige. *Not so much. But if it's crowds you're after, we could always head back to the spaceport. That place is always packed tighter than a Meertori transport schooner on its return trip from the asteroid belt.*

I hummed noncommittally. "That's a little far. Anything closer?"

How about the race dome? said Paige. *That's not far from here, and ever since they retrofitted the arena for Querts, there's been hot action on those shiny, flying buggers around the clock. Whoever colluded with the event staff to bring in the Querts basically handed the arena owners a license to generate their own SEUs.*

"Perfect," I said.

Paige rerouted the car once more.

Carl stared at me. "Care to fill me in on whatever's going on up there?" He tapped his head.

"Simple," I said. "We'll drop you off a few blocks from the race dome. From there, you'll pretend to go on your merry way, but in reality you'll follow us on foot. A few blocks later, I'll exit at the dome proper. The guys tailing us should get off as well. By that point, you'll be in a position to follow them. You can keep an eye on them while they keep tabs on me. Your surveillance information should help us brainstorm a plan of action."

Carl frowned, his bottom lip curling so hard it nearly engulfed the top one.

"What?" I said. "It's a good plan."

"It separates us," said Carl. "Bad things happen when we get separated, as evidenced by recent events."

"Look, just because I woke up delirious next to a dumpster after ditching you doesn't mean I plan to make a habit of it. I'll be fine. Regardless, Paige'll be in constant contact. You'll know exactly where I am and what's going on at all times."

"That's what I thought last time, too." Carl leaned into his seat and crossed his arms.

I sighed and turned my eyes back to the blurred cityscape, the muffled whirr of the cab acting as a buffer between me and my sourpuss of a partner. There was no use arguing with Carl. His protective instincts had a way of overwhelming his otherwise logical sensibilities. I couldn't really fault him for it, though. He had my best interests at heart—or at the cybernetic equivalent of one—but it could still be tiresome to be treated like an eighty-five-year-old child at times.

After a few minutes of awkward silence, the cab pulled over in front of a real estate investments building, its door lifting to allow Carl passage. Bombastic music and effects from the race dome trickled in through the open doorway, bringing with them a wave of warm, Cetie air. As I glanced behind me, I noticed the silver crossover pulling to the side of the street a couple hundred meters behind us.

Carl paused with his hand on the rim of the cab's exit. "You're sure you want to do this?"

"What's the worst that could happen?" I asked.

He gave me a raised eyebrow.

"Don't answer that," I said. "Yes, I'm sure. Just stay close."

Carl left, and the door swung back down. I trained my eyes on the crossover behind us. As the cab whirred into motion, so did the crossover, without anyone having exited.

"So far so good," I said.

You know, I don't always agree with Carl, said Paige, *but he has a point. Do try to avoid hypnotic presentations and psychoactive drugs this time, will you?*

"Wait...are you expressing concern?" I asked. "You're shaken up over losing my Brain signal, aren't you?"

A little, yes.

No snark. That *was* a surprise.

"I'll do my best," I said.

The cab took a corner, shot forward a few hundred meters, and slid to a halt as it hit a patch of race dome traffic.

"Here's fine," I told Paige. "I'll walk the rest."

The cab door popped open, and I stepped into a flood of optical and sonic oppression. The gaudy monstrosity of the race dome loomed farther down the street—an overstuffed, pink hemispherical pimple jutting from the earth, waiting to be popped. Gigantic holoprojectors streamed vids into the air above the dome, showing highlights from the latest match as speakers blared commentary and advertisements at any passersby who might still remain oblivious to the monument's presence.

"—and He Who Walks in the Shadow of Death zooms into the lead, followed closely by Thundering Herd. They're heading into the fire spiral, and it looks like The Wings of Albion is making a move. It's tucking in its wings for a burst—"

Unlike most pedestrians, who stood rooted in place gaping at the spectacle, I walked as I watched, but watch I did, filtering the action through my peripheral vision. The Querts—which resembled oversized hummingbirds who'd had their feathers removed and replaced with scaly, scintillating skin—flapped their wings furiously, ramming into one another from the sides and back as they tilted and shifted, following a course outlined by neon green rings and projected into the sky of the race dome by swivel-mounted holoprojectors. The course changed each match, and the projectors only displayed the three closest upcoming checkpoints in front of the leader, which made for wild flying from the

Querts when the projectors threw in a tight loop-the-loop or helical spiral. To make sure spectators didn't lose interest, the course designers threw all sorts of additional obstacles at the Querts, from spinning propellers to flaming hoops to active high-voltage capacitor plates that crackled with power and fired streams of electricity at unpredictable intervals. The ordeal was entirely unsafe, but the Querts were a few neurons short of sentience, so as long as the event staff organizers kept the trainers' fingers greased, everyone stayed happy.

"—and it's neck and neck. Wings of Albion and Thundering Herd. Thundering Herd and Wings of Albion. They're heading into the Globe of Death. One revolution. Now two. Wings of Albion takes a slight lead and—oh! He's taken a pulse from a Tesla coil right to the thorax. Wings of Albion is down, but he looks to be ok. Yes, he's moving his wings. Thundering Herd surges into first, but Fool Me Twice is close behind—"

As I walked, I kept my head forward, acting nonchalant—or as much as I could while skirting increasingly dense pockets of chatting race fanatics and compulsive gamblers.

"How are we doing, Paige?" I asked. "Carl get a line on the tailers?"

Barely, she replied. *He turned the corner behind us as the crossover pulled away. Looks like a pack of four Diraxi exited the vehicle. One of them is wearing a pair of sashes, like your friend at the Veesnu chapel.*

"Is it the same guy?" I asked.

Not sure, said Paige.

I snorted. "And here I thought you were a master at distinguishing between the hard-bodied buggers."

I am, said Paige with a tinge of annoyance. *But I'd need a closer inspection to be able to tell. Carl, despite his exceptional vision, hasn't been able to get a clear look at them.*

"But they're following me?" I asked.

Yes, said Paige. *They're headed right for you.*

"And Carl's tracking them?"

What do you think?

"Just making sure. No need to get snappy."

I headed across the street, skirting around a pair of cabs moving at a crawl through the race crowds, before stepping into the race dome interior. The arena's foyer spread out before me, bending to my left and right as it followed the curvature of the dome. Lifts and escalators for ushering people to the upper levels dotted the far end, slicing their way between food kiosks and margarita stands, while closer to the doors robo-vendors hawked commemorative sleeveless tees, beer steins, and Quert plushies. Images and vids of the highest ranked champions flashed in the rafters with their win-loss records listed below them, each color coded, with the reigning champion, Wing Gnat, shown in an obnoxious race dome pink. Crowd noise and blaring music surrounded me like a thick fog.

I headed right to a flashing, overlong series of displays showing up-to-the-second betting lines for the Quert contestants in each of the next five heats. Gamblers milled around the screens, some staring intently at the ever-changing numbers, others standing glassy-eyed as they interacted with their Brains, no doubt calculating their own betting odds based off the contest-ants' previous successes.

I glanced over my shoulder, back toward the dome's main entrance. A Dirax head towered over the mostly human race fans, a splash of color from its sash peeking over its shoulders. The alien walked toward me at a measured pace.

"Where are the rest of them?" I asked.

According to Carl, they spread out, said Paige. *It's just your friend from the chapel after you now. Carl's monitoring him.*

I sidled up next to a pair of ventilator-clad Meertori and pretended to study the displays. Within a few moments, I heard a familiar voice booming within my head.

Human. We have things to discuss.

I turned to one of the Meertori and pointed to the displays. "So, pal, what do you think about Lime and Scale? Does he have what it takes? Is that a good line?"

I couldn't see the Meertor's reaction from behind his respirator, but from the way he recoiled I'm sure he thought I was either a thief or a member of the Pylon Alpha gaming commission.

Human. Did you not process my request?

I turned to the Dirax, who stood a bare arm's length behind me. "I'm sorry, are you talking to me?"

My missives are directed to your receptor only. You are the only human who can process my communications.

"Say...do I know you?" I asked. "Are you that guy from the chapel?"

Is this an attempt at jocularity? Are my distinctive sashes not enough of an identifying feature?

"You're right. Sorry. It's just that my brain is a little fuzzy. I passed out and woke up in an alley with a blinding headache. You wouldn't know anything about that, would you?"

We have matters to discuss. Matters regarding a client of yours. Valerie Meeks.

I blinked. How did the priest know about her? I'd never mentioned her, unless I did so while in my apple and rain-induced trance. Surely its knowledge of the connection between us hinted at the brainwashing and mind-reading capabilities I'd suspected the Diraxi had developed.

Or, it connected the dots between you and Carl, said Paige. *Even if it didn't make the cognitive leap between your appearances at his chapel, surely it spotted your partner exiting our cab earlier.*

Paige had a point. I crossed my arms as I stared at the priest. "Alright. Fine. Let's talk."

Not here, came the Dirax's voice. *Somewhere more private.*

I glanced around me. Every gambler's eyes were trained on the displays or were defocused as they watched vids or analyzed statistics via their own Brains. Arena music blasted through speakers, mingling with the ambient crowd noise to form a steady roar.

"We're good here," I said. "I don't think anyone's listening. Besides, you said I was the only one who could process your signals."

I stated you were the only human who could do such a thing. Also, your voice carries, and you appear to have an impulsive nature.

I raised an eyebrow, more at the first part than the last. People had told me I brayed like a donkey.

Apparently, the Dirax was only somewhat familiar with human facial emotions. It took my eyebrow contortions as a signal of disbelief. *If you wish to know the truth about your friend, you will have to place trust in me. Follow, if you please.*

The priest turned tail and headed off through the crowd.

Might as well do as it says, said Paige. *Carl's close by. He's got your feed.*

I'm doing better than that, came Carl's voice in my head. *I've got you in my line of sight. Just don't hop into any unmarked vehicles or huff any weird chemicals.*

Curiosity and the urging of my robotic peers won out over discretion. I followed my tall, Veesnu-preaching compatriot as it sought out rivulets in the crowd through which we could walk. It headed to our left, past the escalators and beer kiosks and robo-vendors into the arena's eastern concourse where the crowds thinned.

An alarm sounded overhead, accompanied by the rapid, auctioneer-like voice of one of the announcers. "Five minutes until the next race, ladies and gentlemen, five minutes. Bets are accepted via Brain right up until start time. Please take your seats."

We continued to walk as the remaining race fans filtered towards their chairs.

I glanced back and spotted Carl a few hundred paces behind me, dodging a pack of lingering race fans. "You mind telling me where we're going?"

A place that will insulate us from prying antennae, ideally one encircled by numerous layers of alternating metals, hydrocarbons, and composite ceramics high in aqueous content.

"Uh...what?" I said.

A room surrounded by concrete and steel. Here. Given the exodus of individuals to the central arena, this should suffice. The Dirax held out a pincer arm in emphasis, pointing to a door emblazoned with a cartoonish image of a standing humanoid.

"You want us to talk in a bathroom?"

The Dirax said nothing, choosing instead to clack its pincers. I still didn't understand the full breadth of that piece of body language. What did it mean in this instance? Annoyance?

Impatience might be more accurate, said Paige. *But close enough.*

I shrugged and waltzed in, the doors zipping open as I approached them. The room forked, a row of a couple dozen stalls and urinals on the left, washbasins and specialty stalls for the more common alien species on the right. I took the left hand side, in case I felt the need to relieve myself after conversing with the sash-clad priest.

"Alright, we're here," I said, turning. "So now can we—awk!"

I meant to say talk, but the pincer flying toward my face changed the situation.

21

I ducked and weaved to the side as the priest's left pincer whistled toward my face, my kick boxer training taking over in the blink of an adrenaline-fueled eye. Sensing the miss, the Dirax cocked its arm for a wicked backhand. I tucked my arms in close to my body, my hands balled into fists and pulled close to my face for protection, and hopped to the side, causing the pincer slap to miss by a good quarter meter. I landed on my left foot, planted on the tile floor, and spun, sending a flying kick into the Dirax's narrow midsection.

My blow connected with a crack as my shin made contact with its exoskeleton, sending the priest stumbling toward the urinals. Pain shot through my leg, but I ignored it. The bone wasn't broken—I knew as soon as I returned the leg to the ground and shifted my stance—so I stored the pain, using it as fuel for my fire. I'd entered full on ass-kicking mode, and my opponent's status as a member of the clergy wasn't about to stop me from unloading on him with every ounce of whoop-ass my two feet could muster.

The Dirax turned and came at me again, lashing out with a double pincer arm overhand elbow chop. I ducked and shifted to the side, knocking its legs out from under it with a short kick jab. It landed flat on its back, cracking the floor underneath where its carapace made contact with the tile. With alarming speed, it flipped over and crouched low, its pincer arms resting near the floor and its back legs tucked up underneath. I backed up and crouched low in return.

The Dirax paused, its eyes trained on me, and I assessed the situation. My opponent had two advantages: its reach and its hard-shelled coating. The reach I could easily counter. The Dirax wasn't particularly quick, and with my low center of gravity, I could easily kick its legs out from under it again and again. The exoskeleton was more of a problem. My shin throbbed from where it had contacted the creature's abdomen, and I wasn't sure how much punishment the alien preacher could absorb before feeling any ill effects.

The priest came at me, scurrying low before rising up, single pincer held high to snap me. I was ready. I delivered a flying heel kick to its face, sending it tumbling into one of the stalls. It fell and crashed into the toilet, sending bits of porcelain into the air as water sprayed from a busted hose.

The fractured chunks of toilet bowl clattered on the tile as they fell, but something else clattered, too—feet. The Dirax's buddies rounded the corners, two from the front of the bathroom near the exit and one from the back. They must've been laying in waiting in the alternative physiology stalls, knowing their sash-clad pal would jump me. How long had I been fighting the tall guy, anyway? And where the hell was Carl?

Paige started to tell me he was almost there, but I tuned her out as the remaining Diraxi converged on me. The pair by the door approached, pincers held open before them, ready for action, while the guy at the back waited for the priest in the stall to get up.

During my halcyon fighting days, inaction had always foretold defeat, so I acted. I feinted toward the lovely couple near the door, causing them to pause. The lone wolf in the rear saw the back of my shirt and lunged for me, hoping to catch me unawares—exactly as I'd hoped.

I spun, jumped, and delivered a flying knee to its exposed skull, putting my full body weight behind it. The alien crashed into the urinals, its head the meat in an unexpected knee and porcelain sandwich.

I darted to the other side of the bathroom, but the priest's friends were quicker than I'd expected. One matched me step for step, pausing at the other end of the sinks, ready for my feints. I crouched, and the cavalry arrived.

Carl burst in through the door and headed straight for the Dirax in front of me, aided, no doubt, by my streaming Brain feed of the events of the past half minute. The Dirax turned at the puff of the door, its pincers raised, but Carl was too quick, and his compunctions about not causing harm only extended to humans. My partner slammed a rigid finger jab into an indentation three-quarters of the way up the Dirax's sternum—the Diraxi equivalent of the solar plexus.

The big insect stumbled and, for lack of a better word, shrieked. It wasn't a vocalization, of course, but I heard the undirected, electromagnetic scream pulse around my head. I dropped to the floor, the soundless yell filling my mind momentarily until Paige blocked the Brain signal. Meanwhile, I heard another thump and crash coming from the other side of the bathroom, most likely as Carl dropped another of the armor-clad aliens of the cloth.

As I stumbled to my feet—the Dirax's subvocal scream had brought my headache back with a vengeance—Carl darted around the corner and grabbed my arm.

"Let's go," he said.

I didn't argue, but apparently the Diraxi had the same idea we did. Before my shoes could get any traction on the floor, the guy Carl had karate chopped in the breastbone surged out of the stall and headed for the exit. Scurrying and clattering footsteps followed from the other side of the bathroom as the contingent of Veesnu warriors fled the scene of the crime.

The chaplain with the sashes exited last. As the door closed behind it, I heard its voice in my head. *Consider this a warning, human. Disassociate yourself from the Meeks woman. Willfully forget your visit to us.*

Carl's fingers dug into my arm from the force of his grip, but they relaxed as the last of the Diraxi left. His face softened as he studied me. "How's your leg?"

"Hurts a bit," I said. "It'll be bruised tomorrow, but I've been through worse."

"And your knee?"

"Miraculously fine," I said. "Apparently it's harder than a Diraxi head."

Water hissed as it sprayed through broken pipes on the other side of the bathroom, the sound mingling with the soft rush of spillover swirling into the floor drains. Carl shook his head.

"Don't say it," I said.

"I wasn't going to," he said. "But you have to admit, coming into an enclosed space like this wasn't the wisest of choices."

"How was I supposed to know the Zen-like Veesnu priest was going to come at me, carapace puffed and claws out? I thought he wanted to talk."

I'll take partial responsibility for this one, said Paige. *I encouraged Rich to follow the guy. I didn't think he'd attack him either.*

Carl and I both startled as a latch clicked in one of the stalls behind us. A Meertor emerged, shaking, the clasps from his respirator rattling in their sockets. He eyed us with a look most people reserved for psychopaths and committers of war crimes. "What in the sulfurous rains of Venus...?"

I glanced at Carl. "Um...we should go."

22

I sunk into my office chair, leaned back, and propped my feet up on my desk. As I did so, a soft, slow moan slithered out of my lips.

"Better?" asked Carl, as he plopped into one of the chairs opposite me.

"You bet." We'd stopped by the house on the way back from the tube station, picking up painkillers, Buzzkills, and a few beers. The combined effects of the three had eliminated my aches and pains, both from my shin and the inside of my head, and released some of the residual tension from my muscles.

Normally, alcohol would've made me drowsy, but I was still wired from my bout with the Diraxi. Instead, the beers had awakened me—or at least a part of me. My midsection growled.

I snapped my fingers. "You know what would hit the spot right about now? A deep-dish pepperoni, mushroom, and feta from DeMarco's."

"Pizza?" said Carl. "Now?"

"Yes," I said. "Paige—make it so."

My digital lady companion sent in the order.

Carl shook his head. "I don't know how you can be so nonchalant right now."

"Why shouldn't I be?" I said. "I took on a quartet of armor-clad, two-meter-plus-tall Diraxi and came out on top. Apparently Rich 'Funny Feet' Weed's still got it." I waggled a foot in emphasis.

"The way I remember it, it was my arrival and swift finger jabs that turned the tide of battle in your favor," said Carl. "And that's not what I'm talking about."

"Then what are you talking about?" I asked.

"The police summons you're most likely going to receive any moment, now."

"Ah. Right."

On our trip back from the race dome, Carl had expounded on his hypothesis for why the Veesnu Dirax had attacked me in the bathroom, which mainly revolved around the fact that local privacy laws prevented businesses from installing security cameras in places where people were likely to expose their genitals. However, the vast majority of the rest of the arena was under surveillance, including the hallway outside the men's room, and the event staff surely knew by now that the Diraxi and I were responsible for the damage to their lavatory.

I, of course, had my own Brain feed as evidence of my innocence in the mêlée, but Carl and I had pored over it together on our tube trip back from the arena, and unfortunately, it was anything but conclusive. Because I'd had my back to the Diraxi priest when he initiated his pincer punch, I didn't have any evidence of his intent to harm me, and his subsequent backhand looked rather out of control when viewed through my feed. The next action by either party was me kicking him in the waist. After watching the feed a few more times, we decided the overall impression of who initiated the fighting was inconclusive—or, at least, it could appear that way to a jury. Besides, even if a jury determined I wasn't the instigator in the fight, I'd still be liable for damages caused and be subject to a hearty fine.

The fact that I hadn't yet received a call from the police, however, meant I might skate away scot-free. Perhaps the arena owners were used to disorderly fans upset by race results and didn't want to have to bother with the police any more than I did. Or, perhaps they saw the burst pipes, wet floors, and cracked bathroom tiles and figured they had nothing to gain from a police investigation and quite a bit to lose from a potential lawsuit. Either way, I felt more at ease about the legal ramifications of my actions with each passing moment.

"I don't know, Carl," I said. "I think my patented Weed family luck is going to keep me out of trouble again."

"Don't be ridiculous," my partner said. "There's no such thing. If there was, you wouldn't have been attacked in the lavatory in the first place. Or woken up in that alley. Or set upon by angry bees yesterday."

"You'll never understand," I said. "You're a glass half-empty kind of guy, whereas I'm the glass totally full sort. Preferably full of something delicious, like whiskey and cola."

"I think your metaphors are getting a little stretched," said Carl.

I shrugged, rolled my eyes, and focused my attentions on something useful—how long it would take for the pizza to arrive. I gave Paige a silent, digital prod.

Relax, she said. *It hasn't even finished cooking, yet. See?*

A progress bar flashed in the bottom left of my field of vision.

Carl tapped his fingers on the arm of his chair. "Why do you think the Diraxi attacked you, anyway?"

"Isn't it obvious?" I asked, shifting in my seat and reversing the positions of my feet on the desk. "They don't want me digging into Valerie's past anymore..."

I paused. In the aftermath of the fight, with my adrenaline surging and blood pounding through my ears, I hadn't spared a thought for my client. As soon as fears for my own safety had receded, they'd been replaced with Carl's concerns for my legal well-being. It wasn't until now, with the various drugs I'd ingested taking effect in my system, that I thought about what Valerie had said to me earlier in the day.

I pictured her, standing in front of my door wearing her paisley leggings and yellow halter top, twisting her fingers together as she glanced over her shoulders. 'There's people after you?,' I'd asked. 'Yes, exactly! The Diraxi,' she'd said. I'd taken her concerns with a grain of salt at the time, but what if she'd meant the statement literally? What if the Diraxi meant her *physical* harm, as they'd meant me? Despite her spectacular, toned abdominals, I didn't get the impression Valerie was the kind of woman who could defend herself against a mob of angry, pincer-wielding aliens.

"Well, of course the Diraxi don't want you looking into Valerie's connection to them," continued Carl, "but the question is why? What secret would be worth physically assaulting someone to hide?"

"I, uh...don't know," I said, my mind heading in a different direction. "Maybe brainwashing technology, like I said earlier. Paige, can we call Valerie? I'm a little concerned about her."

I can try, she said, *but, well...you know.*

I sat expectantly, hoping to hear the distinctive trill of a Brain call, but nothing more than the sound of my own breathing filled my ears.

Paige's voice returned to confirm what I already knew. *Sorry. We're still blocked.*

I frowned and rubbed my brow. "I don't get it. She clearly needs our help. She admitted that much this morning. Why block us from calling her?"

"Maybe someone's monitoring her communications," said Carl, "and she doesn't want a third party privy to her conversations. Or maybe it has to do with that mental blockage you hypothesized."

"Maybe." I drummed my fingers on my desk, my thoughts of Valerie transforming into wild fantasies, including one where she ran through the woods in a flowing white dress as wild-eyed Diraxi chased her, firing electromagnetic prompts of fear and anxiety toward her cerebral cortex.

"Rich?" said Carl.

I blinked and looked up. "Yeah?"

"Did you change the settings on the cleaning bots for your office?"

"No."

"Have you been here without me since we left yesterday?" asked Carl.

"Now, when would I have done that?" I asked. "I've been with you the entire time. Why are you asking?"

"Because I think someone's been in here," he said.

I pulled my feet off the desk and sat up. "Huh? How can you tell?"

Carl pointed to the bronze bust of me that graced the corner of my desk, the one with my professional win-loss record etched into the base to remind me of the glory days. "Your egotistical monument. It's been rotated three hundredths of a radian clockwise with respect to your desk."

I glanced at the statue, pausing a moment to admire my own face. "Really?"

Carl nodded. "I cache all sorts of arbitrary information in my memory banks. Usually it proves useless and I delete it later, but not always."

"So, what? You think someone broke into my office?" A thought struck me. "The same people who tossed Valerie's place?"

"Possibly." Carl stood and moved toward the shelves, sofa, and coffee table that helped my office look like a real place of business. He glanced to and fro, inspecting the curios and knickknacks populating the area. "No. Scratch that. I'd say it's unlikely."

"Unlikely someone broke in, or unlikely it was the same people that trashed Val's apartment?" I asked.

"The latter," said Carl. "Someone was clearly here. A number of things are out of place, but unlike Miss Meeks' residence, the items are only slightly shifted. Whoever was here hid their tracks well. My optical filters aren't detecting any unexpected fingerprints, and if I hadn't recently cached a vid of your office, I wouldn't have noticed."

I scratched my head. Someone had broken into my office, but if Carl was right, it wasn't the same people who'd trespassed on Valerie's property. So who did it? The Diraxi from the Veesnu chapel? Valerie? Who? And why the hell wasn't Valerie answering my calls?

"What's on your mind?" asked Carl, returning to his seat.

"What's on my mind is I'm tired of pussy-footing around. I think it's time we returned the favor someone so generously gifted us. You up for some snooping?"

"Depends on how dangerous and or legal is it," said Carl. "What's your plan?"

"You'll see." I gave my robot friend a wink. It didn't put him at ease.

23

"This is the worst idea you've ever had," said Carl.

"What are you talking about," I said as our cab pulled over to the side of the street. "This plan is foolproof."

"You said something very similar yesterday," said Carl. "Right before you were set upon by angry bees."

I stared out the window at the blocky Veesnu chapel, the sun and neuron projection hovering over the entrance. "Trust me, this is going to work. Now, let's go over the details one more time."

Carl clenched his jaw and looked out the opposite window. "I'm not going to do this."

"Yes, you are," I said.

"And what makes you think that?"

"Because if you don't, I'll have to do it all by myself, and without you, my chances of success plummet," I said. "Given the potential risks involved, you're not going to let that happen. Now, again. The plan."

Carl sighed. "I'll enter the chapel. The greeter at the door should recognize me and ask me to leave. I'll ignore him and race toward the lift, but I won't use it. I'll race down the stairs. Once I reach the basement level, I'll break into the sermon room and take stock of the situation. If a sermon is in progress, I'll make a scene while taking stock of the location and the people who are there. If not, I'll bypass it and keep going. I'll make a rounds of the basement, saving the recording from my visual feed, then head back upstairs and exit the premises. Meanwhile, you'll progress with your part in this doomed arrangement."

"It's not doomed," I said as I rubbed at my face. It already felt hot. "This is totally going to work."

"Unless one of the Diraxi talks to you," said Carl. "I may not be an expert on Diraxi physiology, but I'm fairly sure they'll know you're you if you communicate with them."

"Then I won't talk to them." I took a deep breath and adjusted my robe. "Now be honest. How do I look?"

"Ridiculous," said Carl. "But...more or less like your canvas. If it's dark, people might confuse the two of you."

I smiled. Before returning to the Veesnu chapel, we'd called upon a friend of mine, someone I'd met years ago during my stint as a flightwing instructor. He was a makeup artist who specialized in prostheses for high-budget, techno-thriller vids—the kinds that featured crazy, made up alien races and in which entire star-systems tended to combust as a result of the wild actions of the protagonists. Using my cached Brain feed from when I'd entered the Veesnu chapel the first time, he'd printed me a realistic mask mimicking the facial features of the bald chap I'd spotted inside the church. As long as I didn't make exaggerated motions with my lips or jaw, the mask disguised me perfectly—or at least I thought so. Carl disagreed.

"Don't worry so much," I said. "Between the mask and this stylish navy robe my buddy snagged from the prop department, I look like a dead ringer for our friend, Baldy."

Carl cringed. "Couldn't you have used an adjective other than 'dead?' Are you intentionally trying to make me nervous?"

"Come on, you know the Diraxi weren't trying to kill me at the race dome," I said. "They just planned on roughing me up a little. Scare me. Get me to give up on the case. If they'd meant me real harm, they would've come after me someplace else. Someplace that didn't have cameras pointed at the entrances and exits to all the bathrooms."

"Someplace like this?" Carl pointed at the church.

I snorted. "Ok, point made. But this would still be a terrible place to off me. Paige has the full feed of my actions. If I go in that door and never come back out, I think the cops will know who to blame."

"Yes, but you'd still be dead," said Carl.

"I'll be fine, Carl. I promise. Now go on. Enact phase one of the plan. Paige'll let me know when to move in."

The cab door swung open. Carl looked at me. He hesitated, as if he was going to say something, but he didn't. Instead he hopped out and headed into the Veesnu shrine.

I sat in the cab, drumming my fingers on my thigh. "Alright, Paige. Give me the blow by blow."

No nonsense from Paige. She got straight to it. Perhaps she was worried, too. *There's a Dirax at the front, waiting at the podium. Not the same one who was there earlier, based on the curvature of its anepisternum—*

I didn't ask, and Paige kept going.

—but it's wearing the same distinctive pair of sashes as your attacker. It seems to be aware of who Carl is. It's telling him to leave, and...Carl's off. He's running. He's at the stairs, heading down. The Dirax is yelling. Hold on a sec. Carl's glancing back. Ok, yes, the Dirax with the velvet chest flair is after him. Go.

I gripped the side of the cab, launched myself out, and darted in through the chapel's front doors with all the speed and grace one could expect from a medically-rejuvenated octogenarian kick boxer. The cramped, cylindrical entryway was devoid of life, so I hustled past the podium and down the left hallway.

As much as I'd argued to Carl that my plan to snoop on the Veesnu cultists was solid, there was one giant, gaping pitfall—one I hoped I wouldn't fall into. What if I happened to bump into my shiny-headed body double? I'd taken the left hallway in the hopes Baldy still lingered in the room I'd seen him enter on the right, but I couldn't discount the possibility that I might encounter him. If I did, I had a backup plan—one I hadn't shared with Carl, one that required wit, sophistication, and subtlety: I'd kick the dude in his giblets and make a run for it.

I slowed as I approached the first door on my right. I drew a deep breath as I reminded myself to be calm and act reserved. I stepped forward, and the door blinked open.

The room the door revealed was empty, at least of intelligent life. An austere bed, neatly made with plain white sheets, rested along the wall to my left. To my right, I spotted a plush recliner with a wall mounted projector behind it, and speakers peeked out from alcoves set in the walls—audiovisual systems for Veesnu indoctrination, no doubt. Through a door to my right, I saw polished tile, porcelain, and chrome. A bathroom, most likely.

I stepped out and continued along the hallway. Under different circumstances, I might've partaken in more serious digging, but I was operating under time constraints, and I didn't think rifling through one of the Veesnu disciples' living quarters would provide many clues for my investigation.

"How are we doing, Paige?" I whispered.

Not bad, she said. *Carl's fast, and those Diraxi aren't. I don't think they expected anyone to bust in and run an eight hundred meter dash in their basement.*

The next room I tried mimicked the first, but the third room contained something the other two hadn't— a man, sitting on his bed, wearing khaki trousers and a pleated white shirt with a single buttoned front pocket. He looked up at the sound of the door and blinked a few times. I took a step back, but I was too slow.

"Royce? Hey." He stood and approached. "I haven't seen you in a while. How've you been?"

It was the moment of truth—the time to channel my inner monk. I clasped my hands and responded with a shrug, a slightly tilted head, and a couple of raised thumbs.

"Hm. Yeah. Me, too," said the man. "I've got to admit, it's been difficult these past few weeks. More difficult than I expected. The sermons. The reading materials. The flow of information. It's overwhelming at times. I have trouble remembering it all. Sometimes... Sometimes I think I have trouble remembering other things, too. Did you ever feel that way when you started?"

I shook my head.

"No? I suppose not. You're a natural, from everything I've heard. Speaking of which, I've heard you're on the short list for ascension. Are they that close?"

I wondered what that last part meant, but I nodded.

The mystery man raised his brows and nodded. "Wow. Well...you've earned it. Any advice for the rest of us?"

I took a moment to think that one through, then I brought my arm out and held it toward the sofa chair and projector combo.

"A deeper understand of Veesnu. Yes, of course. Thanks, Royce. Your advice is always impeccable."

I jerked a thumb at the hallway.

"You have things to do. I understand. Well, thanks for stopping by. And good luck."

I nodded and moved on.

Nicely done, said Paige. *Makes me think you should shut up and listen more often.*

I thought of a snappy retort but kept it to myself as the crux of Paige's statement dawned on me.

I knew you could learn, Paige said, reading my thoughts. *Now hurry. Carl can't keep those Diraxi busy for-ever.*

I found a staircase and headed up, taking the steps two at a time. Lady Luck was with me. The corridor I popped into was completely empty. The first door I tried led to a supply closet, but in a twist of serendipity, the second door I tested led me straight to the jackpot.

I stood in a rectangular, whitewashed room that looked like a cross between an oncologist's office and a military command center. In front of me, two parallel rows of translucent, acrylic desks faced the wall, each fitted with a trio of displays and ringed from behind by a bay of holoprojectors. Behind each desk was a padded, high-backed chair—for Diraxi use, based on the tucks in the seat backs. The holoprojectors hung, quiet and life-less, and all the displays gleamed with a dull, matte off-black.

A huge, toroidal machine with white plastic walls and a bed in the middle dominated the other half of the room. It reminded me of a magnetic resonance scanner, but this one was decidedly home-brewed. An additional display—no holoprojector this time—sprouted from a gap in the plastic, and thick, multicolored cables bundled with zip-ties trailed out the gap, along the floor, and up into the ceiling. Next to the cylindrical monstrosity sat a plush recliner chair surrounded by holoprojectors and speakers. A compact integrated medical scanner for measuring vitals stood next to it, and an unopened bag of saline, electrolytes, and nutrients hung from a pole atop it.

As I absorbed my surroundings, I knew I'd found what I searched for while simultaneously having no idea *what*, exactly, I'd found.

"Paige, can you fill me in on what I'm looking at?"

Sorry, champ, she said. *I'm not sure I can add much to what you've already surmised. Though I'll add that whatever you plan on doing here, you need to speed it up. Carl's on his way out.*

"Did he find anything?" I asked as I walked over to the medical equipment.

Nothing quite like this, if that's what you mean.

I poked at the display on the big, cloud-colored machine, then moved my finger to the multicolored cables.

How's that method working out for you? asked Paige.

"Don't knock it," I said. "Poking things with fingers is a time-honored detective tradition. I'm sure many a case has been solved this way."

Seriously, Rich. Move it, Paige said. *We don't have much time.*

I hopped to the display stations. There weren't any manual inputs—at least not any I was familiar with. Below the screens, a couple tong-like protrusions stuck out from the work stations, each with an oblong metal loop attached to the end.

Clawsticks, said Paige. *Like joysticks, but for use with pincers.*

I grabbed one and wiggled it back and forth. The matte dark gray display blossomed to life with a static sun image. A line of text in a language I wasn't familiar with scrolled across the bottom.

"What does that say?" I asked.

It says to sign in for access, said Paige.

"Well? Can you?"

I heard crickets, then, *No. It's Brain-specific. Or Diraxi mind-specific, most likely.*

"Come on. Isn't there anything you can do?"

I jumped as a booming voice—not Paige's—filled the void in my head. *What are you doing here?*

I turned. A Dirax with a pale, blotchy discoloration on the lower left of its jaw filled the doorframe, its eyes and antenna turned directly toward me.

24

I tensed as I spotted the Dirax. My mind raced. Should I play it cool, pretend to be lost, and hope for the best? Rehash the mime routine I'd successfully pulled off downstairs? Or bum rush the tall insectoid, drive a flying heel kick into its solar plexus, and haul tail out of there?

I wet my lips as I stood, words forming on my mouth of their own accord. "I...uh..."

Run! urged Paige.

I took a step forward, ready to follow her advice, but an omnipresent Diraxi voice halted me.

Wait...you are not Royce. The Dirax clacked its pincers, but not menacingly. Almost casually. *Oh, by the nine suns of Contega... You are that idiot the others have mentioned. Weed, correct?*

In my neck of the woods, calling someone an idiot could be considered fighting words, but rather than crouching, pincers out, as the sash-clad Veesnu priest had while accosting me in the race dome bathroom, this

Dirax simply stood there, observing me, its pincer arms hanging loosely at its sides. I took advantage of the opening. I hunched and stepped forward, planting my weight on my left foot and preparing a strike.

You do not understand the magnitude of situation into which you have stumbled, do you? the Dirax's voice came. *You will ruin everything if left unattended. But luck, if such a concept is real, is with you. I retained the closest presence to this room after you sounded the alarm.*

The Dirax's words slowed my attack to an imperceptible crawl. "Wait, what? Alarm?"

The silent alarm present on the workstations. They activate when a foreign mind interfaces with them. They will know it was you. There is no way around it. You must come with me. The others must surely approach now that your friend has completed whatever escapade you tasked him with.

The Dirax turned and walked off down the hall, leaving me standing there, wobbling with my weight on one leg and nothing to kick. The last time I'd followed a Dirax's instructions to follow along, I'd ended up accosted in a public restroom, but something about this particular Dirax's request felt different—probably his references to 'they' and 'the others.'

Don't ask me, said Paige. *Last time I told you to trust one of these guys you nearly got a claw to the face.*

Time pressured my decision. The Dirax booked it down the hallway, and I followed in kind. We passed several rooms, some containing more banks of workstations and medical equipment, others that radiated warmth and hummed with electricity and the sound of cooling pumps for server arrays.

The blotchy-faced Dirax hooked a right, swiveled through a series of interconnected passages, and popped open the door to a stairwell, all at a speed somewhere between a jog and a canter.

I tried to make conversation as we took to the steps. "Hey, do you mind telling me—"

No. Stay quiet. Stay close. Time is short.

We descended to the ground floor and stopped in front of an emergency exit—the old school kind, sporting a push bar and lacking a motion sensor. The Dirax's antennae flickered, and a lock clacked in its socket. My escort shoved the door open, and, before I could protest, he'd wrapped a spindly arm around me and given me a none-too-gentle nudge toward the exit.

"Hey, wait a second," I said as I stumbled into an alley behind the Veesnu chapel. "What the hell's going on here? Who are you? What—"

Be quiet. Leave. And...what is the human expression? Keep your head low. You will be contacted if necessary.

"Hey! I—"

The door slammed in my face, the questions on my tongue left to dry in the balmy Cetie night air.

I rubbed a hand across my face, the tips of my fingers slipping as they passed over the unnaturally smooth surface of the mask. Sweat oozed from my pores and wicked the synthetic material to my face. I loosened the collar of my robe, dug a hand under the edge of the mask, and tugged. It slipped from my head with a slurping pop.

"I don't suppose you have any theories about what the hell's going on?" I asked Paige.

Oh, I always have theories, she responded. *But none of them have much evidence to support them. Certainly not enough to believe in them beyond a measure of reasonable doubt.*

I ran a hand across my sweat-slicked hair before moving it down to my chin, where my fingers met resistance as they passed over the stubby bristles sprouting from the tip of my jaw. In my unplanned morning scramble, I'd forgotten to use the autoshaver. "Perfect. You're like my own personal attorney." I sighed. "Where's Carl?"

He's biding his time in the same alley we found you earlier in the day—the one behind the falafel and burrito shop. He figured the Diraxi wouldn't think to look for him there. It would be too obvious of a spot. He's on his way over now.

I took a deep breath, filling my lungs with air mercifully free of any hints of garbage or urine—or apples and rain, for that matter. I studied the emergency exit—its scratches and gouges, its battered steel and nicked paint—and wondered if I'd exited through it once or twice today. It bothered me that I couldn't remember any of what happened after I sat down at the Veesnu sermon. How had I made it from this alley to the other? Had the blotchy-faced Dirax played a hand in that as well?

You know, it strikes me that perhaps we should follow the pale-jawed Dirax's advice, said Paige.

"Specifically?" I asked.

We need to leave. Who knows when someone else is going to drop by here and have a negative reaction to our presence.

I didn't argue. One alien initiated beating at the hands of exoskeleton-clad cultists per day was enough for me.

25

I sat in a padded, tan-colored booth at Katoh's, my elbows resting on a polished bamboo table. Carl sat across from me. At my right, miniature plates packed with four to six pieces of norimaki, fukomaki, and temaki snaked around the side of the booth, the spin of the conveyor belt's wheels inaudible underneath the low roar of the early-evening dinner crowd. I snagged a plate of spicy tuna and another of sea urchin roe, doused them with a pour of the house soy, and dove in.

Carl rubbed his hands together and cast hungry eyes my way. When he licked his lips, I broke my dam of silence.

"You want one?" I asked.

Carl hesitated, but only for a moment. "Yes. Screw the catch chamber. I'll empty it while you sleep tonight."

"Tuna or roe?"

"Both."

Carl grabbed a plate and I deposited a pair of the seaweed and rice wrapped delicacies in front of him. He popped the roe boat in his mouth and smiled as he chewed.

"Good, right?" I said.

Carl responded with a mixture of moans and nodding. "Mmm. Yes. Get one of those carp narezushis while you're at it." He pointed at the conveyer to a covered bowl with delicate scrollwork on the side.

I grabbed the plate in question. "Wait...is this one of those fermented fish ones? Gross. Keep this one of your side of the table, will you?"

Carl opened the bowl, inhaling the aroma before popping a couple of the foul-smelling rolls into his mouth. His moans became indecent.

I shook my head. "Seriously? You finally decide to eat something and *that's* what you go for?"

Carl swallowed before answering. "I understand your trepidation. Your biology is attuned to certain smells you associate with decay. It's a survival mechanism to keep you from eating spoiled food. But, boy, are you missing out! The fermentation adds incredible layers of flavor and texture to the dish. The chemical detectors in my mouth just went into overdrive to keep up."

I snorted. "Yeah, mine don't do that. And I wouldn't be caught dead eating those things—no pun intended."

Carl smiled as he wolfed down another bite. "Guess you're right. We each have abilities the other could conceivably be envious of. I'm not sure I'm entirely ready to put the enjoyment of fermented sushi on par with fully-realized free will, but it's a start."

"Cheers to that." I held up a cup of sake.

Carl clinked me with a spare chopstick, and we ate in silence. Carl stopped after his lone platter of stinky fish rolls, but I kept going. I polished off an additional three plates before my partner interrupted.

"So...care to bounce ideas off one another?"

"I'm not sure there's much to talk about," I said. "We're at a dead end."

After ditching my blisteringly-hot robe and mask combination, I'd caught a cab with Carl out of Knotting-ton to the tube station, whereupon I'd had Paige give Valerie a few more Brain calls only to be rejected repeatedly. After arriving in Cozy Harbor, we'd booked it to Valerie's apartment, where I found that her front door had been fixed. Whether or not Valerie was home, I couldn't tell, but repeated chime activations, knocks, and calls for her by name didn't rouse her, though they did rouse some neighbors and bring me various threats of violence and police action. From there, we'd headed to Val's bakery, but similar actions there brought similar results. In a fit of inspiration, I'd tried the pass code from the morning on the door, but it no longer worked. Hungry, thirsty, and depressed, I'd settled on Katoh's for some solid and liquid pick-me-ups.

"We're not at a dead end," said Carl. "The information you gathered at the Veesnu chapel could prove incredibly useful."

"How so?" I asked. "All I discovered was that, in all likelihood, both me and Professor Castaneva from the Cetie U biology department are right. Her, in that Veesnu is a combination religion and science, one that involves the use of complicated, home-brewed medical equipment, and me, in that those Veesnu headcases are brainwashing their disciples. Literally. I can't imagine what else those resonance scanners and holoprojector arrays are for."

"To be fair, we're not sure what any of that equipment is for," said Carl. "I'll have to go through your feed later tonight with Paige to see if we can glean any additional clues from what you saw and heard. But it's useful information, even if you weren't able to access any Diraxi data from the displays."

I shook my head. "I don't know, Carl. What if I'm right? What if the Diraxi *are* brainwashing religious 'pilgrims' and Valerie is one of them. It may be immoral, but is it illegal? Valerie accepted Veesnu of her own free will, as far as we know. Why should we interfere?"

"Because she came to us for assistance," said Carl. "As you put it earlier, if she's suffering from mental foul play, some part of her is still lucid enough to seek help. And we agreed to provide it to her. Besides, even if what the Veesnu believers are doing is legal— something we're not sure of, by any means—breaking into Miss Meeks' apartment isn't. Neither is attacking you at the race dome. And let's not forget someone trespassed in your office—possibly the Diraxi. Those are all criminal offenses."

I shrugged and played with the last of my sushi rolls.

"Come on," said Carl. "What about your sermon-inspired blackout? Or the mysterious Dirax at the chapel who helped you escape? None of that interests you?"

I looked up at my pal. Apparently, he took the look on my face as an answer.

"Oh, I see," said Carl. "You're down in the dumps because Miss Meeks won't answer your calls."

"Yes, Carl, I am," I said. "I'll admit it. I'm worried about Valerie. But there's nothing I can do. She won't answer my Brain pings. She hasn't posted to her social media profiles in weeks. We can't find her. I don't know what else to try. And the stuff you mentioned? The break-ins, the blotchy faced Dirax? Yeah, they interest me. But it's been a long day. I'm tired. Right now, I just want to pop a few more Buzzkills and painkillers and go to bed."

Carl grimaced.

"What?" I asked.

"The Buzzkills and painkillers? We left them at your office."

I frowned and shook my head. "We'll stop there on our way home."

Paige paid as I got up to go. After leaving Katoh's, Carl and I caught a cab and headed back to my office, which wasn't as huge a burden as I'd made it out to be. The building wasn't more than a few minutes drive from my apartment.

The entire ride, thoughts of Valerie accosted me. I'd been honest to Carl—to a degree. I was worried about her, but more so than I let on, and on multiple levels. What if the Diraxi meant her bodily harm? She'd implied as much in our last conversation, and if the Veesnu chaplain had tried to injure me, why not her? Surely she knew more about whatever was going on behind the closed Veesnu church doors than I did. If they suspected her of spreading information...

I also fretted over the emotional and mental damage the Diraxi might be inflicting upon her—not only the deleterious effects on her memory, but her overall ability to think, reason, and process information.

The thing that stuck in my craw—the biggest piece I'd omitted from my conversation with Carl—was the effect of Valerie's brainwashing on *me*. Despite my best efforts, I'd fallen for her. I knew that. What could I say? It was more than her physical beauty. She'd paid attention, spoken kindly, and shared a shy smile with me. But—and this was the part that scared me—what if the Valerie I'd come to know was instead a repressed part of her, a personality existing only in a corner of her mind, hidden behind a Veesnu-induced blockade? What if the real Valerie didn't care for me at all? By curing her of whatever malaise the Diraxi had cast upon her...would she forget me entirely?

We reached my office building. I entered and sent for the lift, my thoughts still running roughshod over my senses.

A trill brought me out of my reverie. "Paige...is that Val?"

My digital lady friend had ridden shotgun with me throughout my mental excursion. She said, in almost a sad voice, *Sorry, pal. It's another GenBorn number.*

I sighed. "Seriously? They already called about my appointment earlier today. Decline it."

The lift arrived and Carl and I entered. As the elevator accelerated upward, my Brain trilled once more.

GenBorn again, said Paige, anticipating my question. *It's not the same number that called this morning, if you're curious.*

"Fine, put them through," I said angrily.

I anticipated the onset of the call and launched into a tirade as soon as it connected. "Yes, GenBorn? I'd like to talk to a manager please. I want to change my communication preferences so that—"

The voice on the other end of the line wasn't the kind, secretarial voice that had dialed me in the morning. Instead, it was rough, masculine, and direct. "Don't enter your office."

The lift dinged and the door opened.

"Um...what?" I said.

"Do not enter your office," said the voice. "It's not safe."

Carl stepped into the hallway, curiosity plain on his face. He gave me a silent head nod as if to say, *What's up?*

I followed him into the hall so the lift wouldn't close on me. "What do you mean? Who is this?"

Silence reigned, followed by the familiar, bubbly voice of Paige. *He hung up.*

"Who was it?" I asked.

Not sure, said Paige. *Like I said, it was a GenBorn corporate number. It's not assigned to any one individual.*

Paige had filled Carl in. "Why didn't he want you to enter the office?"

Before I could answer that I didn't know, the office exploded.

26

I found myself staring at the ceiling, hot and wet, as fine droplets pelted me in the face. A red light flashed intermittently—the fire alarm if I wasn't mistaken—but the alarm's distinctive, pulsing blare didn't accompany it. Instead, the roaring of a thousand oceans filled my ears, waves crashing on windswept shores and breakers impacting stone.

Orange and yellow tongues licked the corners of my vision. I tried to shift to view them more clearly, but my neck declined to cooperate, instead rebuking me with a sharp, stinging pain.

Over the oceanic roar, I could make out a voice. A familiar one. Paige's. She was saying something over and over. A name. *My* name. Rich. She seemed upset, or perhaps concerned. I couldn't grasp why. The water was fine, and warm. Oh, so warm—like a sauna.

I felt a shaking underneath me—not the rocking of a wave, more like a mild earthquake. A rumbling. Perhaps the pounding of feet. Leaving my neck and its cranki-

ness alone, I tried to shift my eyeballs from the intoxi-
cating allure of the ceiling and the mysterious, roiling
black cloud travelling across it.

They obliged. I peered down the hallway. I spotted
someone. Carl! Good old Carl, he'd never abandon
me—though he looked busy. He'd made some friends.
Well-dressed chaps in gray suits. Some of them held
long, oblong implements. Batons, maybe? And they
were throwing a party. There were others. Diraxi,
mostly.

I blinked. Actually, just Diraxi. And it wasn't so much
of a party as a mêlée. Diraxi pincers snapped at grey
rayon covered arms, batons flew, and Carl darted here
and there, chopping at carapaces with his bare hands.
He turned and ran toward me, but didn't stop.

I tried to shift my eyes his way as he left my field of
vision, but the squishy orbs in my skull wouldn't cooperate. The hot rain continued to fall, and the pounding
of the waves continued.

A minute, or perhaps only a few seconds, later, Carl
returned. He stood over me, his mouth moving, but no
words came out.

"Hey, Carl, it's good to see you. What's with the
waves and the rain and the roar?" I asked—or I think I
did. My mouth moved. I could feel it.

Carl's lips continued to flap. I wasn't sure what he
was getting at, but his timing was lousy. Didn't he know
I was trying to sleep? I distinctly remembered desiring
that in the near past. With Paige's voice surging in my
mind and Carl's face centimeters from my own, I decided to take a nap.

27

I sat in a hard-backed excuse for an office chair, staring across a desk at a surly sergeant at the local police branch. The man sported a thick horseshoe mustache that he wore over his scowl, and his fingers drummed the surface of his desk with the same intensity as his gaze.

Nearby, a nasally-voiced Meertor proclaimed his innocence to a deputy detective. "I implore you sir, those anhydrous tetrachloride tablets aren't mine. I mean, they are, I suppose, but I didn't know that's what they were. I was just asking that man for a dose of respirator inhalants, as my current stores are running low. He must've slipped them into my satchel when I wasn't looking. Please—"

The sergeant's gruff voice drowned out the Meertor's pleas. "So, let's go over this one more time. For my amusement, let's say."

"Really?" I asked.

"Really."

I sighed. Despite reveling in the joys of an explosion-induced catnap, I'd never made it to bed.

I'd woken up on the sidewalk outside my apartment building. Carl had sat beside me, a worried expression plastered across his face. As soon as he'd seen my eyelids flicker, he'd sighed and asked if I could hear him. I could. The crashing wave-like roar that had filled my ears was gone, replaced instead with a dull, bothersome ringing. I'd tried to nod to Carl in agreement, but my neck took exception to that, so I'd been forced to use words.

My vocal cords had strained, my voice sounding scratchy and faint in my own head as I'd said yes. Carl had sighed, and suddenly Paige had appeared in my mind, asking if I was ok. I thought I was, and I'd tried to say as much, but I'm not sure how much of it came out the way I'd intended. I'd also noted how thirsty I was and asked if Carl could get me a drink of water. He'd said he would, but he insisted I wait until the paramedics arrived.

Above me, tongues of flame licked at the sides of my fourth floor office while firefighting drones zipped around the outside of the building firing water and fire-retardant chemicals in through broken windows. The inferno seemed to have been contained on my floor, though based on the twisting of the steel girders peeking through the smoke haze and the char covering the exterior of the building, some serious damage had been inflicted.

I'd asked Carl how I'd made it to the sidewalk, and he'd proceeded to fill in the gaps in my memory. The blast from the explosion had briefly laid him out as well—possibly damaging a few of his more finely-tuned sensors—but he'd recovered much more quickly than I had. His systems had come back online bare moments after the sprinklers had activated. And that's when the party had started.

A squad of Diraxi had poured in through the stairwell down the hall, none of them wearing sashes, but according to Paige's analysis of Carl's feed, their posture and the prominence of their thoraxes had betrayed their evil intentions. Carl had prepped to defend me, but before the Diraxi took more than a few steps toward us, the door to the office down the hall from me, that of a self-employed financial advisor, had snapped open, spitting out a group of dudes in gray suits. They'd come prepared for trouble. With Carl's help, they engaged the Diraxi, who apparently hadn't counted on the presence of the suit-and-tie clad folks. The alien intruders put up minimal resistance before retreating. The guys in gray had chased after them, and Carl had returned to me. As the fire threatened to grow into an inferno, Carl whisked me downstairs and out to the sidewalk.

I'd asked about the men in gray, but Carl had as little knowledge about them as I did. He'd never considered pursuing them. His entire focus had been on me and my well-being. I'd smiled when he'd told me that. Good old Carl.

At that point, the EMTs had arrived and I'd been whisked to the local outpost of Pylon Alpha General, where I'd been poked, prodded, scanned, checked for burns, smoke inhalation, and popped eardrums, and run through a gamut of concussion and neurological tests. After a couple hours of exciting medical testing, I was diagnosed with moderate cases of whiplash and tinnitus, mild dehydration, and a bruised coccyx from where'd I'd landed flat on my ass. I was given a cocktail of medications and summarily discharged, but my night had only just begun. A nice, scowling police officer had met me at the discharge station and gently suggested I accompany him to the local station for a chat.

From there, I'd taken an all-expenses-paid trip in a lights- and siren-equipped police cruiser to the precinct, gotten my prints and retina scanned, and been introduced to the sunny, lovable sergeant and his pet face caterpillar.

I stared at the man, wondering if his autoshaver secretly laughed at him every morning as it worked around his whiskers. "What do you want to know?"

"Let's start with your office," said the sergeant. "You know, the one that exploded."

"As if there were any other." The officer glared at me. Apparently he didn't appreciate my wit. "What about it?"

"You think the party who set the explosive inside it was...?"

"Isn't it obvious?" I said. "The Diraxi. The Veesnu nuts. From the chapel in Knottington."

"Right. The priests." The sergeant looked at me, his brows furrowed and his lips twisted in ill-restrained displeasure.

"You don't have to believe *me*," I said. "You've got Carl's feed of the whole incident, as well as the one from my own Brain."

"Oh, I know," said the sergeant. "We're analyzing it as we speak, along with other evidence we've gathered.

Such as the surveillance video we requisitioned from the race dome downtown."

"Well, there you go," I said. "Between that and my Brain feed of the incident, you have more than enough evidence to implicate the Veesnu lunatics."

"You mean the feed of you and that fellow with the sashes going at it in the bathroom? You seemed to have given as good as you got."

I knew he'd bring that up. "You know as well as I do I'm the victim here. *I'm* the one whose office was torched. *I* was assaulted. The only reason I didn't report that race dome thing was because I didn't want to be held responsible for the damages to the facilities."

"Riiiiight," said the sergeant. "And I'm sure your choice not to report the fight had nothing to do with your subsequent trespassing at the Veesnu chapel."

"I didn't trespass," I said, folding my arms.

"Oh, really? Explain that to me."

"The church is freely open to anyone who wishes to visit it," I said. "I'd already visited it before and been welcomed with open arms—or, open pincers, as the case may be. I simply decided to pay the place a second visit. No one at any time indicated to me I wasn't welcome there, nor did they ask me to leave."

"At least, not until the arrival of this one Dirax with the...what did you call it?" said the sergeant. "The blotchy face?"

"That's right," I said.

"And he wasn't upset with your snooping?"

"I was lost," I said. "And no he wasn't. He escorted me to the exit in a kind and efficient manner."

The police officer continued to drum his fingers on the table. "And the reason you think this is all happening, the reason you think this pious batch of Diraxi is after you is because...?"

"I know how it sounds."

"Humor me."

I didn't think humoring the man was possible. Not in his current state. "Because I've discovered they're medically altering people's minds. They're brainwashing them, preparing them for some weird mystical journey, and turning them into true believers of Veesnu."

"Like they did with your current client?" asked the sergeant. "One Valerie Meeks?"

"Correct."

"The one who claimed not to know you? And won't return your calls? And who you can't find?"

"Yes. Possibly because she's been kidnapped," I said. "You should look into that, by the way."

"Duly noted." The sergeant held up a hand. "Hold on, I've got a call." He leaned back in his chair, eyes defocusing. "Hmm? Yes. Yes. No. Nothing? You're sure? And who authorized that? He did? Oh. I see. Alright then. Yes, I understand."

The officer sat up and turned his moustache back in my direction.

"Who was that?" I asked.

"None of your business." He continued to glare at me, without elaborating.

I got tired of waiting for a prompt. "Um...so what happens now? Are we done here?"

"*I'm* not done," said the sergeant. "Not by a long shot. I have a ton of work to do to wrap up this disaster, thanks in no small part to you. But you, the lucky dog that you are, *are* done. As much as I'd love to send this mess crashing down on your head, I don't have enough evidence to charge you with anything, and your private investigator's license shields you from some of the more minor claims I could file against you. But if you so much as sniff that chapel in Knottington, or any of the other Veesnu locations in my jurisdiction, I'll slap you with so many obstruction of justice and tampering charges your head will spin. Got it?"

"Got it." I stood. "What about the Diraxi, though? What happens to them?"

"They're my problem, now," said the sergeant. "But if you're concerned about your safety, don't be. We have them in custody awaiting questioning, and the bomb squad just finished checking out your apartment. It's clear. I've even been asked to dispatch a squad to keep tabs on your neighborhood until everything clears up."

I rose an eyebrow. "You've been asked? By who?" Was that what the call was about?

The officer stared at me as he ran a thumb and forefinger over his fuzzy piece of face décor, his lips motionless. I would've appreciated an answer to the question, as well as answers to numerous other ones that milled about the recesses of my mind, but it didn't look as if I was going to get any satisfaction out of the policeman. I headed for the exit, sending a ping to my partner as I did so.

28

I found Carl waiting for me on the street corner outside the station. We shared a wordless moment—mutual looks of relief that I was neither dead, severely injured, or imprisoned. My luck held steady as we headed home, as I managed to avoid getting tailed, attacked, or having anything in my general vicinity spontaneously combust.

I didn't let myself fully relax until my feet lay firmly planted on my welcome mat and I heard the front door to my apartment zip shut behind me. I took a deep breath and sighed.

"Home sweet home, huh?" said Carl.

"Let's say I would've been *very* upset if it were this place instead of my office that had been blown to smithereens," I said.

"Want to grab a bite or have a sip of something with a kick?" said Carl.

I shook my head. "Even though it feels like an eternity since I deposited that sushi into my gullet, I just want to get to bed."

Carl nodded and headed toward the wrought iron spiral stairs. "I'll walk you up."

"I'm not a child, Carl," I said. "I can put myself to sleep."

He paused with a foot on the first step and turned to look at me. "Right. Sorry. It's one of the curses of being an android. I still remember when you were a babe in my arms as if it were yesterday. Sometimes when I experience high levels of external stress, I forget it's been eighty-five years. Well, not forget, precisely, but—"

I clapped my old friend on the shoulder. "I know what you mean, bud. And thanks for everything you did today. I wouldn't be here without you. Literally."

Carl nodded, a hint of a smile curling the corner of his lips. "Anytime, Rich." He clapped me on my shoulder in turn. "Goodnight. Sleep well."

"Goodnight."

Carl headed toward the kitchen, perhaps to take stock of the groceries, while I headed up to my room.

Paige's bubbly voice accosted me while I walked. *Aww... That was a sweet moment.*

"Feeling left out?" I said.

Paige tickled my Brain, the closest she could come to a playful bat of the eyes. *Don't worry, Rich. I know who you really love.*

I rolled my eyes.

Once I got to my room, I sat on my bed, bringing my knees up so I could peel off my shoes and socks. As I stood to take off my shirt, I noticed something on my nightstand—something that hadn't been there when I'd left in the morning.

I let my shirt fall back down to my sides. "Oh, you've got to be kidding me. How many times am I going to have my personal space violated today?"

Paige analyzed the contents of the nightstand using the visual feed from my Brain. *Well, on the bright side, it's not a bomb.*

A stack of Veesnu cardslips, perhaps two dozen or so, rested on the corner of my bedside table. On first glance, each appeared to be identical, featuring the distinctive sun and neuron logo I was starting to wish I'd never have to set eyes on ever again.

"What's on them?" I asked. "Anything special?"

Nope, said Paige as she interfaced with them. *They all hold the same Veesnu proselytization spiel you've heard a couple times now. Want to see it again?*

"Not really." I picked up one of the cards and held it between my fingers. The surface was rough, as if it had been scratched with a pick or blade. I held the card to the light and realized the scratches were actually words. I grabbed another off the pile and inspected it. Same thing.

I scrunched my brows. "What the..."

Wait, said Paige. *Maybe it's a letter.*

"There are numerous letters," I said.

Not letters, genius. A letter. Before the rise of digital communications, people communicated by writing each other missives on pieces of paper or parchment or on stone tablets. It's unorthodox, but I suppose you could do the same thing on plastic cardslips.

"Stone tablets?" I said "Really?"

You need to brush up on your history, said Paige. *Now shut up and read the thing.*

Figuring I had nothing to lose, I sat back down on my bed and held the first card up to my face.

Dear Rich,

I looked up. Dear? Who was this so-called letter from? Valerie? If so, what did she mean by such an introduction? Did she have feelings for me?

Focus, Rich, said Paige. *'Dear' is a standard salutation for these sorts of things. Eyes back on the cards.*

"Right." I tried again, picking up one card as the next ended in an attempt to turn the stack of cards into a coherent, flowing missive.

Dear Rich,

If you're reading this, then you've found my antiquated attempt at communication. I wish there was an easier way for me to contact you, but unfortunately, my circumstances dictate an unconventional strategy in that regard. I wish I could communicate with you directly via more modern methods, but, for reasons I'd still rather not discuss, I was, and still am, simply unable to do so.

Before I go any further, let me first express my sincerest, most profound apologies for how this situation unfolded. Know that I never intended for you to come to any physical harm, or for you to suffer any undue emotional distress as a result of my actions. I mean that from the core of my being. If I'd known my visit to you yesterday morning would take you on the journey it did, I never would've come to you in the first place.

With that said, I must admit, I did intentionally mislead you in regards to my initial appeal. As you may have already guessed, I placed the arcade token in the sock drawer of my apartment with the intent that you'd find it and follow the path on which it took you. But I sorely misjudged where that path would lead, and that's my fault. If only you'd found my fourth and final clue, I'm certain you'd have resolved everything in a much simpler fashion, but you didn't, and so here we are. All I can say is I'm sorry.

And now I come to the part of this letter I've been dreading—the part that pains me as much as it may pain you. Knowing full well that doing so may result in further physical and emotional distress for you, I must still ask that you continue your investigation into the Diraxi practitioners of Veesnu. What they do is an abomination and a condemnation of free will, and as much as it may have benefitted me personally, I cannot in good faith condone their actions any further. They must be stopped. To allow them to continue on their path is to risk the death and suffering of many individuals—more so than just you, Rich. As much as I care for you, I must consider the well-being of others, as well.

And know that I do care for you. I don't know if you sensed it, but when we first met, I felt we had a connection. I thought a spark existed between us, however small or fleeting it may have been. Perhaps I'm imagining things— despite my appearance, I'm not as experienced in matters of the heart as you might imagine—but that's how I felt. And that's why it pains me so much to ask you to stay the path you're on.

I don't know if I'll ever see you again, but if not, know that I'll always care for you, and that I'm confident you can unravel the mess I unwittingly created for you.

Sincerely,
Valerie

I set the last of the engraved cards on my bedside table. I turned my eyes to the floor, stared at the carpet, and blinked a few times.

You...want me to send a recap to Carl? asked Paige.

"Um...yeah. Sure," I said.

I sighed. I felt content, relived, and confused all at the same time. Content because it turned out Valerie reciprocated my feelings toward her. I wasn't crazy! Relieved because Valerie was safe and sound—or at least she had been at the time she'd scratched her letter into the stack of cards. Her writing hadn't betrayed any hints of distress, and she hadn't mentioned anything that made me think she might still be in danger. And confused because I still had no idea what my lovely client was talking about for the most part, or what the Diraxi were up to. And what in the world did Valerie mean by her 'fourth and final clue?'

As I considered the very real possibility that I might never see Valerie again, or cash in on her promised bounty of delectable bear claws, I heard the front door chime.

29

Carl met me at the front, Paige having filled him in on the contents of the message. He flanked me as I instructed Paige to open the door.

The hard plastic barrier winked open, and outside my apartment stood two individuals: one, a Dirax with a distinctive pale blotch on its jaw, and the other, a man in a tailored gray suit with close-cropped brown hair and an air of formality. The latter's face looked familiar, as if I'd seen him before, but where? I didn't recall getting a good look at any of the men who'd fought the Veesnu Diraxi in the aftermath of my office's explosion.

"Well, I know who *you* are," I said to the Dirax as I turned my eyes to his buddy. "But you...wait. I know where I've seen you. You were in the coffee shop this morning before I stopped by Valerie's bakery."

The man in the suit nodded in acknowledgement. "I'm Marshall Douglass. My friend here doesn't have a given name, which makes introductions difficult, but I call him George and he doesn't take offense to that."

I do not care for names, came the Dirax's voice. *But I do understand their importance in a culture where spoken commands may be interpreted by anyone within range of the pressure wave.*

"Mind if we come in?" said Marshall.

"Who are you guys?" I asked, my face scrunching up in confusion. "Despite where I first met you, George, I'm assuming you're not one of the Veesnu chaps. Are you police?"

"Not quite," said Marshall. "I'm an employee of GenBorn. George is with RAAI Corp."

That's when I placed Marshall's voice. "Hold on. You're the one who called me. Right before my office exploded."

The gray-suited one nodded again. "Correct."

"You want to explain what the hell's going on?" I asked.

Marshall extended a hand into my apartment's interior. "I'd love to, but...may we?"

I nodded and let them in, ushering them toward my sitting room. They sat down, as did Carl and I. I could tell my robotic pal felt an urge to offer them something to drink, but I shot him a small, silent shake of my head. Answers first, booze later—depending on the quality of the explanation.

"So," I said, making myself comfortable on the divan. "Based on who you work for, where I met George, and what I've gathered about my own case, I'm going to assume you two are corporate spies."

"At GenBorn, we refer to my division as the information division," said Marshall.

"You can call it whatever you want. Industrial espio-
nage, snooping, theft. It's all the same to me." I shifted
my eyes from Marshall to the Dirax and back, but the
pair of cucumbers played it cool, so I gave it to them full
force. "Alright. Let's cut to the chase. Clearly you guys
have been keeping tabs on me, and on Valerie. You
know something I don't, and I'm guessing you're here
to share. So tell me...what the hell do GenBorn and
RAAI Corp have invested in religiously-driven brainwashing, and how deep is Valerie Meeks involved?
How bad off is she?"

*I believe you have misinterpreted the specifics of the situa-
tion,* sent George, *and you appear to have a skewed perspective of the parties involved.*

"Huh? How so?" I asked.

"The practitioners of Veesnu aren't involved in any
sort of brainwashing," said Marshall, "and the person
you've come to know as Valerie Meeks isn't precisely
who you think she is."

I blinked. "What do you mean? Is she a spy, too?
Operating under a pseudonym?"

"Not exactly," said Marshall.

I ran my tongue over my teeth and gave the dude a
look. "If you want me to understand what you're talking
about, you're going to have to back up and shoot a little
straighter."

*How familiar are you with consciousness transfer theory,
Mr. Weed?* asked the Dirax.

"Is that a thing?" I said.

*It is. You are a recipient of proprietary GenBorn rejuvena-
tive services, are you not? Have you ever considered why such
a thing is necessary? Why not exist in a separate form alto-*

gether? Your kind has already developed the technology to create sentient systems that exist in perpetuity.

"You're talking about androids," I said. "Like Carl."

Correct. Would it not be beneficial to exist in synthetic form? This is the crux at the core of consciousness transfer theory. It has been a topic of discussion among scientists of numerous species for millennia, but has never been fully realized, primarily because none of us, my species included, have ever been fully able to understand what sparks the creation of a consciousness, much less how to transfer one from an organic to a synthetic mind. But this has not prevented parties from the attempt.

I recalled a discussion I'd had with the sash-clad Veesnu priest as he'd shown me to the sermon. I'd asked about a term he and others had mentioned repeatedly, the Ascension, and he'd said it was a religious test to unleash the spirit and free it to a nebulous, timeless state. *It is a journey of the mind,* he'd said. I'd assumed he'd meant it in the figurative sense, but what if he'd meant it literally?

"Wait." I leaned forward, my brain lingering on the cusp of something important. "Are you suggesting the Valerie I've come to know...is an *android?*"

"Yes," said Marshall. "But what George told you is true. No one has ever been able to fully realize the transfer of a consciousness from an organic mind to a synthetic one, and that statement remains true to this day."

I took a deep breath and settled back into my chair. Valerie? An *android?* My mind raced in a million different directions all at once, but I forced myself to exude at least a measure of composure. "I'm still confused."

"I don't blame you," said Marshall. "I'll try to help you through it. You see, the Diraxi have been working on consciousness transfer methods for a long time. I've been following the subject indirectly for years—George almost as long—but that's only a fraction of the amount of time the Diraxi have committed to the subject. All the leaders in the fields of neural mapping and inter-connectivity are Diraxi, and many of them are also believers in Veesnu, as you might suspect given the tenets of the religion."

Much respected research is being performed by my kind on this subject, sent George. *But even the most knowledgeable members of the community readily admit consciousness transfer is still not possible given current understandings of science. This is why it was so surprising when we discovered rumors of a breakthrough originating from the local practitioners of Veesnu, none of which are renowned scientists, but many of which are known as zealous extremists. At the time, my colleagues and I were investigating reports of unlawful importations of android frames, a clear patent infringement. But those reports also mentioned physical modifications of the frames to make them more similar to local physiologies. Between those two pieces of information, the dots became connected, as the saying goes.*

"George infiltrated the local Veesnu branch to discover what was going on," said Marshall, "but despite his best efforts, he couldn't uncover the new breakthrough that had supposedly been made. As we investigated on our separate ends, the Veesnu increased recruiting, luring people with promises of Ascension, one of which was Valerie Meeks. Then George found something."

I discovered references in the local Veesnu servenet to immersion rates and neural fluxes. These are terms typically associated with activation of a blank cybernetic android mind to a state of consciousness. At this point, we had a suspicion as to the Veesnu believers' plans, but we had to confirm them.

"Which we did, when the Veesnu Diraxi attempted to implant Valerie Meeks' consciousness over that of a blank cybernetic host as it was being activated," said Marshall. "This subject's been proposed in scientific literature but never tried for ethical reasons. The theory is such a procedure would result in the transfer of memories, personality traits, emotional biases and the like, but not actually a transfer of consciousness. Instead, it would merely affect the creation of the new cybernetic consciousness, creating a clone, if you will, while leaving the original consciousness intact in its organic host."

This is precisely what happened with Miss Meeks, sent George. *She was sedated and placed in a neural scanner— one of the white machines near which I found you at the church. An unactivated android designed to mimic her was brought in and a consciousness transfer was attempted, but a delay in the imprinting of Miss Meeks' mind over the blank canvas caused the Diraxi engineers to think the process was unsuccessful. However, the mind did imprint. It merely took time for the new cybernetic mind to adjust to the situation— which was a precarious one. The new android Valerie came to as the original Miss Meeks was being wheeled out of the room, still sedated but clearly alive and well. However, the android Valerie believed she was the original. To see herself laying there was a shock. Frightened and confused, she fled and escaped the facility.*

"This is roughly where you come in, Mr. Weed," said Marshall. "Shortly after her escape from the transfer facility, the new android Valerie Meeks sought you out. But to understand her actions, you have to understand she wasn't the same as her organic counterpart. The new Valerie had the same memories and personality as the original, but this essence, if you will, was imprinted over a stock RAAI Corp cybernetic brain, one designed for compassion, intelligence, and infused with the standard decision-making algorithms all androids have, including your friend here." Marshall pointed to Carl. "The android Valerie saw herself as an individual, but she also possessed a strong desire to protect the original Valerie, who she saw as her owner, from physical and emotional harm.

"She reasoned, quite logically, that the Veesnu practitioners' plan wasn't to transfer the original Valerie's consciousness, but to copy it to her, the clone, and convince her the transfer *had* occurred, making her *feel* as if she'd ascended. But to make the story convincing, a loose end would have to be tied."

The original Valerie would have to die, sent George.

"Exactly," said Marshall. "And the new Valerie couldn't have that. She felt a driving need to warn the organic Valerie that her life was in danger, but she feared by confronting her, she'd risk serious emotional damage to her owner, not only from seeing her own cybernetic clone and knowing the transfer had failed, but also in revealing the intents of the religious mentors in which she'd believed and trusted. She considered going to the police, but again her desire to protect the original Valerie from emotional harm impeded her.

She knew that by involving the police and telling them the truth, the Veesnu consciousness transfer scheme would become public, and Valerie would become the poster child for the entire mess."

George flicked his antennae at me. *The synthetic Valerie decided the best course of action, the one that would ideally protect her owner's physical and emotional well-being the fullest, was for an unassociated third party to discover the scheme of their own accord and put a stop to it. That way, Valerie's life would be saved, and the emotional turmoil upon her would be minimized because she would not see the downfall of her church as stemming from her actions, especially if she never found out about the existence of her clone.*

I took another deep breath and dug my fingers into my temple as I tried to process everything I'd been told. "And I, of course, am the unassociated third party. All the clues Valerie—err, I mean, *android* Valerie—left me were so I'd discover the consciousness transfer scheme and reveal it for what it was worth."

"That's right," said Marshall. "But android Valerie made a couple miscalculations. The first was in thinking she needed your assistance in uncovering the scheme at all. She had no idea we—" He jerked his thumb between George and himself. "—were already involved. And she sorely underestimated how quickly relations between you and the Veesnu Diraxi would deteriorate, something we didn't take into account, either. I suppose none of us realized just how fanatical the Cetie sect of Veesnu believers is. We didn't anticipate they'd plant a bomb in your office and attempt to kill you simply to keep their scheme under wraps."

Thoughts and concerns swirled in my head like a churning maelstrom, and I briefly wondered if the doctors at Pylon Alpha General hadn't been wrong in clearing me of a concussion diagnosis. "Do you, uh...mind if I ask you two a few questions?"

"By all means," said Marshall. "We'll answer if we can."

"The break-in that occurred yesterday at Valerie's apartment," I said. "That was the Diraxi?"

Marshall nodded. "They began pursuing the android Valerie as soon as she escaped, but she was hard to find, even for individuals with, should we say, special talents and limited qualms about breaking the law."

"What do you mean?" I asked.

Android Valerie is an illicit droid, one activated outside the jurisdiction of RAAI Corp, sent George. *She was not connected to the servenets. If she were, she could have been tracked. Likely, the Veesnu planned to transfer the real Valerie's Brain connection to her to keep the android's presence hidden from authorities.*

I recalled the scrawled message in the cardslips upstairs. *I wish I could communicate with you directly via more modern methods, but, for reasons I'd still rather not discuss, I was, and still am, simply unable to do so.* It explained so much. Why Valerie had always shown up to speak with me in person. Why she'd knocked instead of using the Brain activated chimes. And, of course, why she'd never answered my Brain calls—because I'd been calling the real Valerie, who didn't know me. Which reminded me...

"The real Valerie Meeks," I said. "What's she been up to these past couple days?"

"She's spent most of her time at the Veesnu chapel, relaxing and recuperating," said Marshall. "Though she made a trip to her bakery yesterday—"

"—afternoon," I finished. "Of course."

The one interaction with Valerie that didn't add up. That's why she acted the way she did. She didn't lie to me. She didn't forget me. She'd never met me at all. Every other interaction I'd had with Val had been with the android version of her, who I'd believed to be the real Valerie. Those were the interactions with the sweet, tender, caring Valerie—the Valerie, I realized, that was predisposed to like me due to the same subliminal algorithms that made Carl care so deeply for me.

Our connection, the spark Valerie had mentioned in the missive on the cardslips, was a lie, forced on her by her cybernetic brain. I swallowed back my pride and continued. "Ok. Moving on to today. Who broke into my office?"

"What do you mean?" asked Marshall. "The Diraxi from the church did. They planted the bomb."

"I wasn't born yesterday," I said. "You know what I mean. Earlier in the day."

Marshall and George shared a look, and George responded. *You should be grateful for that. If we had not bugged your office, we would not have known when my brethren planted the explosive. Our surveillance saved your life.*

"Is that *all* I should be grateful for?" I asked.

"Pardon?" said Marshall.

"A while ago, when I left the police station," I said. "The sergeant wanted to eat me alive. At least he did—

until he got a call. I don't suppose you two had anything to do with that."

Our employers have deep pockets, sent George, his antennae flickering, *and are active contributors in both tax revenues and campaign contributions. The local arms of Gen-Born and RAAI Corp would like to keep this series of events quiet. Which brings us to one of the primary reasons we have called upon you. We are willing to offer substantial compensation in SEUs in exchange for your silence on this matter.*

"Save it," I said. "You guys saved my life, and kept me out of jail. I don't need your money. But I do have one more question I need answered."

"Ask it," said Marshall.

"How do you know all this?" I asked. "And I don't mean the stuff you garnered through surveillance. I'm talking about the stuff you know about Valerie. How she felt, why she ran, why she contacted me. That."

I anticipated the answer before it left the gray-suited man's lips. "Because she's in our custody. She told us everything."

I ground my teeth as I posed my next question. "So what happens to her now?"

"Nothing adverse, if that's your concern," said Marshall. "We found her, talked to her, and convinced her the best course of action was for her to join GenBorn and put her unique, hands-on knowledge of memory transfer to good use by helping us research methods that may some day facilitate true consciousness transfer between sentient minds."

"How magnanimous of you," I said. "And I suppose GenBorn will also be happy to keep all the profits when it someday adds consciousness transfer to its array of services."

The shoulders of Mr. Douglass's suit jacked bunched as he shrugged.

It was also determined, sent George, *that it would be best for Miss Meeks to continue said research off planet. We agreed with the android Valerie's assessment that her continued presence in Pylon Alpha could cause emotional distress to the real Miss Meeks should the two ever meet.*

"And we wouldn't want your bosses to look bad in any of this either," I said. "That might necessitate more hefty campaign contributions."

That is an additional concern, sent the Dirax. *The android Valerie is already booked on an upcoming flight out of the system set to leave in about ten standard hours. She did say to send you her regards.*

I turned my eyes toward Carl, who'd sat there, unmoving and silent during the entire discourse. I'd almost forgotten he was there. "Is there anything you want to ask, old pal? Or add, for that matter?"

He shook his head. "I think you've covered everything. Unless you'd like to ask the kind gentlemen to compensate you for your lost bear claws."

Part of me wanted to laugh, but my heart wasn't in it. Not this time. "That's your cue to leave, friends."

Marshall and his Dirax companion got up, and I walked them to the exit.

As Marshall left, he paused and turned to me. "If you ever have any questions, or need anything, don't hesitate to ping me. We would've nailed those Veesnu crazies on some charge or other eventually, but in your own unique way, you certainly helped us wrap up our investigation in a neat bow."

"Being almost blown up is a specialty of mine," I said.

Marshall smiled. The blotchy-faced Diraxi didn't, but then again, he didn't have teeth.

I let the door close and returned to the sitting room to Carl.

My friend held his hands in his lap and massaged his fingers together. "You want to talk about anything?"

"Not really," I said.

"Fair enough." Carl waited a moment, probably to see if I'd add anything, but when I didn't he stood. "So...bed then?"

I shook my head.

"I thought you were ready to collapse."

"I was," I said. "But that was before I read Valerie's letter, and before the corporate crew arrived. Now...I'm rather awake."

"You need time to think," said Carl.

"It's not that," I said. "I mean, yes, I do. But there's also something I have to *do*."

"Oh." Carl raised his brows. "Well, by all means, let's go."

"Not us, Carl. Me."

Carl looked at me, *really* looked at me, then nodded. "Alright. I understand. Just be safe."

"I will. See you soon."

30

My feet carried me across the floor of the space-port's epsilon concourse, third level, a thin poly-ethylene-coated bag clutched in my right hand. Crowds surged around me, oblivious to the late standard hour plastered on displays every fifty meters throughout the concourse. Nasal Meertori chuckles emanating from underneath tightly-clasped respirators merged with the disgruntled clacking of Diraxi pincers and the constant drumming of feet and hooves and tarsal claws on the metallic spaceport floor. A light chemical smell hung in the air, that of cleaners and pine-scented air fresheners, trying but not quite succeeding in masking the musk and sweat and body odor of the swaths of multi-species and multi-racial travelers having completed their inter-stellar voyages.

As I dodged a pack of Diraxi, a familiar sight came into view—the façade of Keelok's Funporium, with Kee-lok's creepy smiling muzzle hanging from a sign over the entrance. In the middle of the concourse, on a bench facing the arcade, sat a woman wearing a pale yellow bolero jacket and matching shorts paired with a simple, white blouse. Blond hair with a hint of saffron hung across the side of her face as she stared at the floor, her knees bouncing up and down with nervous energy.

I walked up. "Mind if I sit?"

Valerie looked up. "Rich! What are you doing here?"

"Looking for you, what do you think?" I sat, despite her lack of an answer.

"But how did you know where to find me?"

"Let's say I had a hunch," I said.

Valerie smiled, the warm caring smile I'd first spotted on her face yesterday morning, not even two days prior. The moment seemed as if it happened an eternity ago, but the smile looked the same as I remembered it.

"So...it seems you're a better detective than I gave you credit for, after all," she said. "You missed my fourth clue, but you found me."

"You overestimate my skills," I said. "I've found a lot of detective work involves bumbling around until you stumble into the pieces that don't fit. Keelok's was one of those. And besides, I already checked the waffle shop."

Valerie's smile grew, and she placed her hands in her lap over her now still knees.

"Aren't you going to tell me about the clue I missed?" I asked.

Valerie bobbed her head. "At Professor Castaneva's office. Her cardslips."

I raised an eyebrow. "Yeah, I remember. What about them?"

"The one in the front," said Valerie. "It wasn't one of Francis Castaneva's. Shouldn't have been, anyway. I snuck in while she took a bathroom break and replaced it with a different slip, one for Jörgen Karlson, Professor of Philosophy. He's Cetie U's premier expert on consciousness transfer theory."

I recalled the slips on Fran's desk. I'd noticed the Cetie U logo on the front and assumed they'd belonged to Professor Castaneva. I snorted. "Hah. I'm going to blame that oversight on Carl. If he can cache the rotation of the bronze bust in my office, he should be able to notice an errant name on a cardslip. So tell me...why Keelok's?"

Valerie shrugged. "I don't know, to be honest. After I escaped from the Veesnu temple, I ran back to my apartment—err, I mean, Valerie's apartment—and tried to figure out what to do. I knew I couldn't stay, so I grabbed a pay slip and headed to the spaceport. I figured no one would look for me here. As I wandered around, I stumbled across Keelok's place. I couldn't play any of his games because I hadn't been connected to the servenets yet, so I gave that old arcade cabinet of his a spin. I didn't last very long, but I guess Keelok took pity on me. He gave me another couple tokens on the house."

I snorted. "You're kidding me. That guy? He didn't give you the spiel about his kids starving to death?"

"What can I say," said Val. "Maybe my feminine wiles worked better on him than your charms did."

She tucked a loose strand of hair behind her ear with a delicate finger. As I watched her do so, I had a feeling she might be able to charm just about anyone, of any species. Perhaps my gaze lingered too long, because Valerie turned her head to me and broke the silence.

"So you found my message," she said.

It wasn't a question. She knew I had. "The one on the cardslips. Of course. And I talked to your new friends at GenBorn and RAAI Corp, too."

Valerie gave me a pained sort of look, one with sealed lips and sorrowful eyes.

"That was sarcasm," I said.

"I figured as much," she replied. "But it's for the best. Really. I can't stay here. Not with the real Valerie still alive and well—and, thankfully, blissfully ignorant."

"I know," I said. "And I agree. You need a fresh start, which is an odd thing to say because you started fresh a few days ago."

"It doesn't feel like it to me," said Val, casting her eyes back to the floor. "Feels like a couple hundred years."

I twisted my lips and scratched my neck. "So...how are you holding up?"

"Alright," said Valerie. "It's been a rough adjustment, both mentally and physically. I remember Valerie's life—*my* life—perfectly, as well as she does, I'm sure. I recall what I did, how I acted, how I felt about things. And I *am* her, in so many ways. I feel a rush of emotions when I knead dough or smell the scent of freshly baked bread wafting from a warm oven. I love yellow and white—" Valerie gestured to her outfit. "—even though I have no idea why. And as ridiculous as it may sound, I have a fascination with obscure religions, including Veesnu, despite everything that occurred.

"But at the same time, I'm *not* Valerie. I have thoughts and feelings and emotions I know didn't exist in Valerie's mind. Something drew me to Keelok's Funporium, for example. I got such a thrill out of playing that dopey old arcade game. Valerie never felt that way. She never had any desire to play games at all. And there's other things, too. I know who Valerie was. I wouldn't call her particularly kind or empathetic, and yet—"

"You are," I finished.

Valerie looked at me again, her eyes round and her brows ever so slightly furrowed. I knew we'd get to this part of the conversation. It was inevitable. But I'd prepared myself for it.

"It's the base-layer programming in your cybernetic mind," I said. "All androids have it. It makes you predisposed toward compassion, intelligence, and kindness. It makes you want to protect people and helps you see the best in them. Even in...me."

Valerie smiled and shook her head. "No."

"No?" I said.

"No," said Valerie. "I refuse to believe that. I refuse to believe I'm not in control of my own thoughts and my own beliefs. I care because that's who I am, not who Valerie was, and not who some engineer in a factory thinks I should be."

"I think I've had this conversation before with Carl," I said.

Valerie touched me on the cheek. "I like you, Rich. You're a good guy. And I'm sorry I dragged you into this mess. Maybe that emotion does stem from programming hidden somewhere in the recesses of my mind. But it doesn't define me. Know how I know that?"

"How?" I asked as I lost myself in her eyes.

"Because part of me *isn't* sorry. Part of me is glad I stopped by your door yesterday morning, because it meant I got to know you. Even if for a fleeting instant."

Valerie returned her hand to her lap, and we sat in silence. I felt like I should say something, but I'd never been very good at that, and I didn't want to stick my foot in my mouth and ruin the moment.

"So..." Valerie eventually offered. "What's in the bag?"

I perked up. I'd almost forgotten about the small bag in my hand. "Ah. Well. See for yourself."

I opened it and held it out for her.

Valerie gasped. "Éclairs! You remembered!"

I nodded.

"Where did you get these?" she asked.

"There's a bakery on the way from the tube station to the spaceport," I said. "I've never tried yours, so I can't compare quality, but these are pretty good. I've had them before."

There were two in the bag. I pulled them out and handed one to Valerie.

As the pastry slid into her hand, her face fell. "Oh. But..."

"Don't sweat it," I said. "My partner has the same compunctions. Just eat it and enjoy. You can always empty your catch chamber later."

Valerie smiled. "Alright."

We quit jawing and put our mouths to good use. Smooth buttery vanilla custard hit my tongue as I bit into the éclair, mixing with the sweet yet bitter dark chocolate icing in my mouth. In a few short bites, the experience was over. I licked my lips, liberating them of any frosting trying to make a break for it, and Valerie did the same. Once done, I took Valerie's pastry liner, crumpled it with mine, and returned the pair to the now empty bag.

"That was delicious," said Valerie. "Thank you."

"Anytime," I said.

I leaned back on the bench, as did Valerie, and together we watched the passersby: short, squatty Meertori, shiny Diraxi, humans of all shapes and sizes and colors, and a fair number of droids, from fully-equipped androids to the dumbest of service bots. We silently enjoyed one another's company for a good long while—fifteen or twenty minutes—until at last Valerie spoke.

"Well...I should get going. Interstellar flights always take at least six hours to board, and I wouldn't want anyone, man or machine, getting upset with me for being late."

Before I could respond, Valerie leaned over and planted a soft, tender kiss on my cheek.

"Goodbye, Rich," she said. "I'll miss you."

She stood to leave. I tried to think of what to say, but all that came out of my mouth was a simple, "Bye."

Valerie gave me a smile and a small wave, then turned and walked away. I watched her go, my eyes reflexively dropping to watch the seductive wiggle of her rump.

Paige's voice filled my head. *That was such a touching moment...until now.*

"What," I said. "I'm a man. I can't help myself."

Even when she's an android?

"Believe me, for the first time in my life, I'm tempted," I said. "But no. In this particular scenario, a kiss on the cheek was the perfect happy ending."

I stood and tossed the empty polyethylene bag in a trash receptacle.

So, said Paige. *Now what?*

"Now?" I said. "Now I can finally go to sleep—which I'm going to do right after I give that chicken game at Keelok's one last try. That pathetic high score of mine's been bugging me ever since we left yesterday."

Paige laughed, and I couldn't help but crack a smile, too.

ABOUT THE AUTHOR

Alex P. Berg is a mystery, fantasy, and science fiction author, a scientist, and a heavy metal aficionado. Connect with him at www.alexpberg.com. If you'd like to be notified when new books are released, please sign up for his mailing list on his website. You will only be contacted when new books come out, your address will never be shared, and you can unsubscribe at any time.

Word of mouth is critical to author success. If you enjoyed this novel, please consider leaving a positive review on Amazon. Even if it's only a line or two, it would be a *huge* help. Thanks!

www.ingramcontent.com/pod-product-compliance
Lightning Source LLC
Chambersburg PA
CBHW022156260626
47155CB00019B/3056